The Roar of Morning

The Roar of Morning

De morgen loeit weer aan

TIP MARUGG

TRANSLATED FROM DUTCH BY PAUL VINCENT

YALE UNIVERSITY PRESS ■ NEW HAVEN & LONDON

A MARGELLOS
WORLD REPUBLIC OF LETTERS BOOK

Published with assistance from the Dutch Foundation for Literature.

N ederlands
letterenfonds
dutch foundation
for literature

The Margellos World Republic of Letters is dedicated to making literary works from around the globe available in English through translation. It brings to the English-speaking world the work of leading poets, novelists, essayists, philosophers, and playwrights from Europe, Latin America, Africa, Asia, and the Middle East to stimulate international discourse and creative exchange.

English translation of Dutch text and afterword by Paul Vincent
English translation and afterword copyright © 2015 by Yale University.
Originally published as *De morgen loeit weer aan.* Copyright © 1988 by De Bezige Bij.

Yale University Press books may be purchased in quantity for educational, business, or promotional use. For information, please e-mail sales.press@yale.edu (U.S. office) or sales@yaleup.co.uk (U.K. office).

Set in Electra and Nobel types by Tseng Information Systems, Inc.
Printed in the United States of America.

Library of Congress Control Number: 2015930850
ISBN 978-0-300-20764-4 (paperback : alk. paper)

A catalogue record for this book is available from the British Library.

This paper meets the requirements of ANSI/NISO Z39.48-1992 (Permanence of Paper).

10 9 8 7 6 5 4 3 2 1

CONTENTS

The Roar of Morning

ONE

I live on a core of sedimentary and igneous rock surrounded by coral reefs, part of the arc of islands that encloses the Caribbean basin; on clear afternoons I can see the outline of the mountains on the northern coast of South America. I'm not as young as I was, and on occasion I give myself over to that solitary gratification which the good friars back in school used to call self-abuse—a practice that, as I knew even then, flies in the face of all that is right and sane.

It's about an hour and a half past midnight. I sit on the paved terrace in front of my house and watch the low hills opposite me descend in serried ranks towards the coast. During the day they are grey, but, now, through the magical effect of night, they are shrouded in a mysterious bronze-green veil. Attached to the façade of virtually every house scattered across the nearby slopes is a bare neon tube, and from this distance they look like giant straw-coloured glowworms gnawing at the walls with gently undulating movements. When there is a moon, you can make out the wrecked cars strewn around the houses like so many fossils, not decaying, but eternally waiting. My loyal bitch Fonda lies at my feet and now and then licks my toes slowly and obsequiously through my open slippers. In my garden, six yards or so to the right of where I'm sitting, there's an old indju tree, a giant bowed by the wind. At irregular intervals it lets out a rasping moan, very like the dull, subdued growl that occasionally issues from the throats of old men. There is an unsightly kink in the trunk and the bark is covered in thick brown veins, formed by the sticky sap secreted by the tree. A worn-out veteran who knows he has grown too old and hasn't bothered to clean up after his last ejaculation.

An ugly neon tube shines from the front of my house too. To my left on the terrace there is a small tumbler of whisky with a splash of lukewarm water—my fifth—and to my right the umpteenth bottle of ice-cold Dutch beer. For me they make the ideal combination, with an invigorating effect that I unfortunately discovered only late in life. Lager makes me languid and gloomy, whisky makes me aggressive and gloomy. By alternating these Scottish and Dutch derivatives of barley I often achieve the effect I look for in drink: of creating myself anew.

Every self-respecting citizen must have a front garden. That's the custom around here. Even though the houses might be surrounded by the carcasses of discarded refrigerators, washing machines and cars, which serve both as status symbols and as breeding grounds for the dengue mosquito, the garden must be kept clean and tidy; any weeds must be destroyed immediately. As with certain other things, I have gone my own way. My cluttered, overgrown plot may compare unfavourably with the immaculate gardens elsewhere in the neighbourhood and probably invites critical comments, but I never hear them because I have hardly any contact with other people. I'm not a plant lover exactly, but I do enjoy the feeling of security that the tall bushes around my house afford me. My garden looks rather wild at the moment, as the rainy season has only just ended. Maybe I shall have to do something about it after all. It's amazing how every year a different plant takes over. How these new species get into my garden is a mystery. The oddity currently is a thorny shrub that has grey-green leaves shaped like half-moons, but with the two extremities forked like a snake's tongue; the stems are adorned with gleaming red fruits the size of a pea. Such a beautiful plant can only be poisonous. The emaciated goats that occasionally manage to sneak in here leave it untouched. Which may be why it's running riot. The four trees against the fence on the left look particularly majestic, I think. Like soldiers on parade, they stand in a dead-straight line; they have no lower branches and rise a good twenty feet straight into the air, their thin trunks at once elegant and gross, like the gangling legs of a young goat, as frail and tough as all life.

People who know me, and those who don't, accuse me, not without a touch of envy, of being a recluse who doesn't give a damn about anyone else; they say I have removed myself from all contact with the outside world in this sparsely populated western part of the island, not even allowing a telephone in my hermitage. In fact, my house is on a fairly busy main road, although there are no cars passing at this hour. If I step on it, in twenty minutes I can be in town, where I visit the supermarket frequently, the bookshop occasionally and the barber two or three times a year. And my lair can't be that hard to find, because I get more visitors than I would like.

This afternoon Eugenio dropped by. With his extravagant beard, parted in the middle from lower lip down to Adam's apple, clothes that flap around him because they are several sizes too large and a straw hat with an enormous brim that almost conceals his diminutive figure, he is not an appealing sight and most people avoid him, although they know he's harmless. For about fifteen years he taught the third class at the primary school in the village and organised sports for the children after lessons. It all started one Monday morning when he appeared at school with a stubbly growth of beard, and thereafter he never shaved again. In the space of a few weeks he lost an alarming amount of weight. When he began to keep his big hat on even in class, ceased to talk to his fellow teachers and started giving sex instruction instead of the usual language and math lessons, the headmaster had to act. Eugenio spent three months at the psychiatric clinic in town. Since his discharge, he has been either on sick leave or suspended on full pay; at any rate, he collects his teacher's salary without fail each month. He now lives with a black woman who is twenty years his junior and has an exceptionally fine figure.

Sometimes he shouts obscenities at the packed tourist buses that drive past, and he likes to talk about the dreadful disasters that the astrologers wish upon mankind; as he does so, a fearsome look comes into his eyes, as if he were keen to start scourging himself. But in general he is very friendly. He talks about Abraham Lincoln as if he were still alive, and insists that we all have a double who will breathe his last at the same moment we do. He likes artificial flowers, because although they lose their lustre, they never in fact fade; and now and then he mutters something about hidden drawers full of secret documents.

The secret documents are actually in his boots. He wears calf-length boots that are too big for him, stuffed with pages torn out of books and folded very small. Most of the cuttings contain grandiose pronouncements by people like Churchill, Ortega y Gasset, Gandhi and Fidel Castro, but there is also, for example, a short dissertation on how to prepare a herbal remedy for syphilis, a list of proverbs mentioning cows or dogs, a colour photograph of a half-naked Marilyn Monroe, and the recipe for a hot sauce made of curry, garlic, sweet peppers and onions.

Though he may be a little unbalanced, Eugenio sometimes says things that make you think. "The inhabitants of this island are all scared stiff of walking in the rain. But the fools don't know that it's not the rain but the sun that they should be protecting themselves against." Or, "That was an odd sermon the red-haired priest gave. As if he was addressing the rebellious descendants of the ancient Batavians and was unaware that his congregation in fact consisted mainly of the descendants of Angolan slaves." About a fortnight ago I spent the whole afternoon drinking on the terrace with this oddball. He started talking about Nostradamus, and when I didn't react he switched to the Revelation of St. John the Apostle. My suggestion that the two of them should get together and swap prophecies shut him up completely and we went on drinking in silence, which is the best way to drink anyway. Then, when dirty streaks of grey and pink appeared in the western sky and it began to get dark, he handed me his empty beer bottle and said, "One more beer. Then I must be off." As I went to take the bottle from him, he did not let go immediately. He hunched up his body so that he practically disappeared beneath his hat, and as we both clung to the green bottle he muttered, "You're playing a dangerous game. You sleep all day and stay awake all night. That's unnatural and asking for trouble. You can't protect yourself from perdition solely with drink. If you must be alone, you should at least fill your nights with daydreams."

This afternoon when he walked solemnly through my gate, I was burning rubbish in an oil drum nearby. He stopped and watched me without saying a word. This indicated that I had to say something.

"You look like a walking toadstool with that bloody hat on."

He didn't react, but said, "Today's not a day for burning rubbish."

"Why not? Is it Friday the thirteenth?"

"The wind's blowing from the wrong direction."

"That makes no difference if you do it in an oil drum."

"But you're standing on the wrong side as well. Your clothes and your hair might catch fire. That was a good poem."

"What are you talking about?"

He dropped onto his right knee, untied his left bootlace and took out a neatly folded piece of paper the size of a five-cent coin. He stood up and offered it to me, but from the opposite side of the oil drum from where I was standing. I moved round to the other side and took the paper from him. I unfolded it and read: "After my death—and this will be a comfort to me—no one will be able to find in my papers a single explanation of what really made my life worth living; no one will be able to find the key inside me that explains everything . . ."

"It's not a poem. It's a diary entry by Kierkegaard."

He quickly took the piece of paper out of my hand with a rather offended expression and said, "You shouldn't say Kierkegaard, but

Kièr-ke-gòr. It's written Kierkegaard, but you pronounce it Kièr-ke-gòr."

"Thanks. Now I know."

He dived into his boot again and produced another cutting, which he unfolded before handing it to me. It was my poem about Lilith, the first woman, that had been published some time previously in the weekend supplement of a local daily.

"Why do you think it's a good poem, and why do you keep it?"

"It's a wonderful poem."

"Why do you think it's wonderful?"

"Why do you ask stupid questions?" You think a poem's wonderful because you think it's wonderful. End of story. But you're conceited—I expect you want me to sing the praises of your writing."

"Do you want to come in for a drink?"

"Oh no, never again. Those four animals of yours aren't dogs, they're wolves. But if you'd like to get me a bottle of beer, I'd really appreciate it."

I got him a bottle of beer. He took a short swig, tapped his hat with the neck of the bottle in a kind of military salute, turned on his heel and minced off in the direction of the village.

Now, as I sit here in the night gazing stupidly at hills that keep changing their shape—a game they will continue until morning breaks, when they will resume their original outline—I am overcome with feelings of both pity and admiration for Eugenio. This planet is one huge mess. Jews kill Muslims, Catholics blow up Protestants and the incumbent of the White House who's acting the screen role of president of the United States is heading straight for a confrontation with the Russians. Lies and calumnies, falsifications of the Bible and history have made the world incomprehensible, and you wonder whether there's any possibility of rising above the chaos. But lo and behold! Suddenly a little bird sings, and in this forgotten corner of the world that small action gives us strength because it makes things fall back into place: my poem in a madman's stinking shoe.

A dearth of drink obliges me to go back inside to replenish my supply of Dutch courage, but soon I'm back in my old place under the neon strip, on the same lukewarm paving slab, flanked by my fresh provisions.

At moments like this, when there is not a breath of wind, the night speaks with a chorus of primeval voices: the vegetation in my garden pants, as if the densely planted bushes were gasping for breath; the indju tree moans; the tiny, nameless creatures that forage for food only when it is pitch-dark make rustling noises; far off, an exhausted goat with its head caught in a fence utters a death rattle. Now and then I hear the strange cry of the small birds of prey that come at night to soar in wide arcs on the thermal currents rising from the seaward slopes of the hill: a high-pitched trill, like the giggle of a young girl, immediately followed by a protracted wail, as though the birds are in mortal danger—a moment's happiness smothered by sadness. Just before sunrise, when they should be totally exhausted, the birds fly back to the coast of Venezuela where they live. Sometimes unidentifiable noises can also be heard, whisperings that seem like some incomprehensible warning. But none of these sounds, or even the shooting star high in the sky, manages to shatter the silence and imperturbability of the night which swallows up everything.

I love the hushed quality of the island when nature has fallen asleep, a few hours after midnight when the immobility of darkness prevails. The leaves hang motionless from the trees like tired eyelids. The trailing branches of the milkwood trees, which during the day flirt with the wind and climb up the telegraph poles across the road, have now ceased their coupling manoeuvres and droop loosely like dead snakes. The sky is black apart from an exceptionally large star here and there. Perhaps it will rain soon. When I was a boy I imagined that the darkness was square, four black walls that formed not so much a square as a rectangle, inside which everything was dark. When I was sent to bed and turned out the light, my room was enclosed within a small square. But there was still a narrow strip of light shining under the door, and now and then I could hear a voice or some other sound in the house.

Later, when the other lights in the house had gone out and the bright strip under the door had vanished, the whole building was enclosed in a large square of darkness. Even then there were faint sounds, inexplicable noises in and around the house, and the barely perceptible sighs that I sometimes thought I could hear in the distance. Not much has changed. The boy who used to lie on his narrow bed listening to the sounds of the darkness is now an old man sitting on his terrace gazing at the dark. The square has become larger: the whole Caribbean is surrounded by four black walls of China, and within them damnation continually smoulders.

I don't know if it is a warning that my arteries are becoming clogged with cholesterol, but sometimes at this hour, when the alcohol has gone to my head, I have the urge to play Caribbean Man, or at least make an amalgam of all my fellow inhabitants of the archipelago and dissect them frantically. It is not the Jew but Caribbean Man who is the most tragic figure on earth; his destination is not Auschwitz but Disney World. He lives in hiding, even though the colonial occupation ended long ago. He suffers from night blindness and cures himself by spending the whole day in the sun. His life, a feast of laughter and dancing, is actually a lament, intoned to the sound of calypso, reggae or merengue: his mistrust is fed by disillusionment and the inexorability of fate, by a fundamental scepticism about the likelihood of happy endings. This coconut mentality makes his very existence a web in which he is increasingly entangled. The white man isn't white and the black man isn't black; both are aliens in this land where their umbilical cords are buried.

Eugenio is right. If you try to fill the night with drink alone, you end up fretting about problems that are insoluble.

Around three in the morning, when the silence is intense and the night is at its loveliest, the cockerels start their din. When I was a child, they told me at school that the cockerel flaps its wings and cries cock-a-doodle-doo to greet the sun. That is pure fantasy: the creatures start their hideous concert when it's still pitch-dark and do not stop until it is broad daylight. At the first cockcrow my conscience starts to feel remorse because, unlike other mortals, I am still up at this ungodly hour. Then I quickly clean the glass and the bottle and hurry indoors. But it is at least another hour before I turn in, for I have to follow the nightly rituals to the last detail. The three male dogs must be taken for a walk, for between ten and fifteen minutes each. It must be done separately, or they will tear each other to pieces; having a vagina, Fonda is the only one on good terms with them all. Of course the dogs should have been let out long ago, but I don't like them barking and dashing around when I'm sitting outside. Another end-of-day ceremony is cleaning my teeth. I do this meticulously, brushing upwards and downwards as well as forwards and backwards, then rinsing with a mouthwash that reeks of the hospital. All this is designed to banish the foul aftertaste of drink and cigarettes so that I can go to bed cleansed. The last item on my daily schedule is to take the pistol out of its hiding place in the wardrobe and place it on the table to the right of my bed.

I'm in bed at last and switch off the reading lamp. Then I lie in the small square of darkness as I used to. I reach out and take the pistol off the bedside table. The metal has gone cold quickly because of the air-conditioning. "Birds die in the blue of morning too," I say, or think, and pull the trigger. Apart from the four dogs, no one will probably hear the shot. I have no near neighbours and at this hour there are no pedestrians on the road.

But I usually fall asleep quickly and without any problem, only to be overwhelmed by imaginings that seem to be the visual equivalent of the sounds of the night accompanied by my musings. A dense flight of ugly waterfowl with long legs and retracted necks crosses the plain on the north coast and sails low over the great boulders, whose whimsical, eroded shapes give them the look of massive tombstones. Snakes poke their slimy heads out of the crevices in the cliffs and scrutinise their surroundings through narrowed eyelids; they press their snouts into the ground and slide slowly forward, so that the horny layer covering their bodies is sloughed off; hundreds of cast-off snake skins are left to stink among the rocks. Small, thickset creatures with stubby tails bend themselves double and spit saliva onto the sack-shaped reproductive organ that bulges from their rectum. From a bay choked with driftwood and empty plastic bottles toxic fumes rise, and on the surface of the dead water millions of tiny creatures float, entangled in slippery threads to form a mass of purple jelly. Blue-black fish flap sluggishly about in the mud near the springs that well from the rough limestone. Then, like a speeded-up film, these become mere snatches of images: a long claw with three toes and pointed nails—a thick, rough coat—branching horns above a protruding snout—grooved teeth with poison seeping down them—a leering head with mobile, protruding ears—callused, hairless patches on a rusty-brown coat—prehensile feet like a giant's hairy hands . . .

It sometimes happens, though, that at about three, with the advent of the crowing cocks and the gnawing conscience, I manage to allay my fears with a stiff shot of whisky and decide to stay outside and wait for the sunrise. That means, of course, that I have to fill at least two hours with drunken philosophising, but it's worth it.

When the sun comes up, I have to change my position so that I can look eastwards. I sit on the projecting rim of the big flower pot, in which weeds, not flowers, flourish.

There follows the ritual duel that puts an end to night. The bronze morning light seeps hesitantly through the resisting darkness, and the hills stand out more sharply against the sky, like reclining goddesses with drawn-up knees and enormous breasts. Then the peaks are surrounded by a halo of silver and the tropical sunrise explodes triumphantly over the landscape, a glittering tidal wave of light rolling down the slopes. In these few dazzling moments each day, I think in my drunken way, the heavens warn man of the hell-fire awaiting him.

In a few minutes the miracle is complete. The sun now climbs quickly into the sky and casts sharp contrasts of light and shade across the island.

TWO

Birds die in the blue of morning. I've never heard anyone talk about it, or read anything about it, so I assume I'm the only one who knows about a phenomenon that takes place at every sunrise on the southern slopes of the Great Mountain, when birds dive deliberately to their deaths against a sheer cliff face.

I have observed this strange spectacle four times now, and each time it has moved me deeply. In order not to be seen by the birds, you must conceal yourself well before daybreak, because the transition from dark to light is swift, and after that it takes only a few minutes for the birds to emerge from the trees in the valley below. From such a high vantage point the sunrise is a rather different experience than from my terrace. First you see the hazy black of night, deep in colour to start with but quickly turning to a bluish glow that is drawn across the landscape like a semitransparent veil. Low in the eastern sky, faint streaks of greyish white and pink appear, but are soon dispelled by the first rays of the sun, which hesitantly define the outlines of things and then drench the whole landscape with white light, bringing it to life. At that moment the birds burst out of the treetops with piercing cries and fly upwards with violent wing beats. The sound of their communal screeching can be heard from far away. Suddenly they fall silent, and for a moment they appear to be hanging motionless in the sky. But then they shoot forward, resuming their shrill cries, and dive at great speed towards the cliffs, the sunlight gleaming on their yellow heads and bright green wings. Just before they hit the wall of rock, they bank sharply and soar upwards, grazing the edge of the cliff and heading east towards the new sun. But two or three of the birds do not break their headlong descent or soar upwards: they swoop on towards the cliff and are dashed to pieces against it.

Each time I witness it this spectacle seems absurd. Firstly there is the contradiction of the magnificent birth of a new day and the suicide of the birds, creatures that for me epitomise nature. Then there is the abrupt way in which the birds about to crash break off their aggressive screeching at the sun, without leaving so much as an echo. Yet when I sit tipsily on my terrace in silence and darkness, and the night, oblivious to the emptiness and melancholy of mankind, is populated with monsters, before the cocks have crowed, I am amazed that the scene with those birds makes such an impression on me: haven't I always, even as a boy, associated the dawn with death?

In my nocturnal reveries I have often puzzled over the antics of the birds at the Great Mountain. At first I decided it was an optical illusion, as science knows of no species of bird that practises self-destruction. In the whole animal kingdom, in fact, there are very few examples of animals taking their own lives: voles will drown themselves en masse if they have become too numerous in a particular habitat and conditions are unfavourable; and according to local superstition, scorpions will give themselves a fatal sting if they are in mortal danger and cannot escape. But I quickly reject the idea that I was deluding myself. I wasn't drunk when I observed the spectacle—and I had seen it not once but four times.

Another hypothesis that seems to me more plausible is that the birds crash to their deaths not because they want to commit suicide, but because they suffer from some biological defect, such as the blindness common in older birds. The inbuilt radar that warns them of obstacles in their flight path may have malfunctioned, or they may have suffered paralysis of the wing muscles during gliding, so that they are unable to gain sufficient height in time.

A third explanation, and one I tend to prefer, is that the self-destruction *is* a conscious decision taken when the birds are no longer capable of mating.

For all we know, this phenomenon may have some biblical connotation that mere humans are unable to fathom. After all, the scriptures abound with birds of all kinds. Moses warns the people not to make "the likeness of any winged fowl that flieth in the air," and in his strictures against adultery the author of Proverbs talks about a bird "that hasteth towards the snare, and knoweth not that it is for his wife."

The Great Mountain, as its name crudely suggests, is the highest peak on the island. Its northeastern slope, on the windward side, has been fenced off and declared a national park. On Sundays tourists come to picnic and gawp at the green gourds and the white and purple orchids. The leeward side is very steep, and inaccessible because of the dense vegetation and the piles of boulders. Only the heroically inclined climb to the summit from this side. I'm one of them, though I have never actually reached the top. I stop halfway, because that is where the birds give their early-morning display.

Perhaps it's time to go and see the birds again; it must have been six months since I was there.

On that occasion I left home at about three in the afternoon after the usual set-to with the dogs. I was going to be away all night, so they had to be fed. But it wasn't their usual feeding time; all four left their food untouched and stared accusingly at me as if I had betrayed them. I hoped that as soon as I had gone they would pounce on the liver, their favourite dish, because if they didn't the ants would make short work of it and the dogs would go hungry until the following morning. In fact, the animals started playing up the moment I put my shoes on. The few times a year that I wear shoes to go into town they start yelping in chorus because they know I'll be gone for several hours.

But finally I was ready to leave. On the seat next to me was my old briefcase, stuffed with: a woollen blanket (it can be freezing at night up there among the stars), a half-bottle of whisky (also to keep out the cold — but not a full one, as I did not want to be drunk when I saw the birds, and because I needed to keep a cool head for coming down the next morning — real climbers know that the descent of a mountain is often more dangerous than the ascent), a torch (only to be used in emergencies), a few sandwiches (if I didn't eat them I could always crumble them up for the birds), a thermos filled with ice-cold pineapple juice (for the thirst and the after-thirst), a reserve packet of cigarettes (just imagine dying for a smoke in the wilderness in the middle of the night!) and a tube of red ointment (the label claimed that it had a soothing effect, promoted the healing of cuts, grazes and other injuries to the skin and was also nongreasy, a nonirritant and soluble in water). When I worked in town I used the briefcase for papers and books, but I had converted it into a rucksack with the help of two old belts, because when you climb mountains you need not only both legs free, but also both hands.

It took only twenty minutes to drive to the Great Mountain. I turned off the asphalt road onto a sandy track, which after a few hundred yards became bumpy and gradually narrowed until it finally ceased to exist. I parked the car, hiding it as well as I could among some tall bushes. On this island unattended cars are often stripped bare; everything that can be removed, unscrewed or ripped off is taken. I didn't lock the doors, because there are also some high-minded thieves around who are only after money. They rummage through your car and if they don't find any cash, they just go away. But if all the doors are locked, they feel obliged to break one open.

I strapped the rucksack to my shoulders and set out in good spirits for the foot of the mountain. Outside it was even hotter than it had been in the car; there was scarcely a breath of wind. The sun was halfway across the western sky, at the point where its heat is even more blistering than when it is at its zenith around noon. The terrain was not easy to negotiate: everywhere there were deeply gouged dry river beds dotted with prickly pears and low thorny bushes. I also had to pick my way between the stumps of hundreds of saplings that had been illegally felled for use as fence posts. Everywhere I heard the rustle of lizards; at each step I took, tiny brown creatures darted away. The larger specimens were a dirty blue colour with white patches. I saw no rabbits, although they are plentiful on this mountainside. However, I did find some shallow burrows, skillfully camouflaged and usually containing a litter of three blind young. Nor did I see any deer, although occasional sightings are reported by keen amateur naturalists.

The ground now began to rise steeply and became more wooded: indju and wabi trees that can be found everywhere on the island; paintwood trees with their fantastically fluted trunks; the shorter gourd trees with violet flowers on both branches and trunk, their graceful boughs swaying this way and that suggest a beautiful long-haired woman walking in the wind; and here and there a solid and graceful candle tree with its shiny evergreen leaves. And of course cactuses everywhere, with their vicious spines.

It was a slow and arduous climb. The mountainside was very steep and I had to be careful not to slip. Had I fallen, I could have broken an arm, a leg or even my neck—but at the very least I would have been pierced all over by scores of cactus spines, which break off agonisingly in your flesh. I had already acquired several grazes on my arms and legs, but they were not serious. In the very steep stretches I grabbed a sturdy bush or branch and hauled myself upwards. There were boulders everywhere, but they did not help much. They all looked grey, but when I grabbed hold of one of them, its surface turned out to be so rough that it tore open the skin of my hand, whereas another rock that looked just the same turned out to be so slippery that I could not get a grip on it.

Halfway to my destination I noticed that the vegetation had changed yet again. The prickly pears and columnar cactuses gradually thinned out, and I saw more and more globular cactuses, which soon started to dominate the landscape. There were a few splendid specimens: ribbed spheres adorned with neat ranks of spines and surmounted by a white-haired phallus with pale red flowers. But most of them just looked like some prickly animal that had rolled into a ball. I also saw trees whose names I did not know, some of them swarming with yellow parasites, as well as huge trees that were leaning over at an angle of forty-five degrees but still had not fallen. In an enormous columnar cactus, also leaning precariously between heaven and earth, I saw the nest of a warawara, in the inaccessible site these birds of prey always choose. I reached my destination at about six.

I was exhausted from the climb and needed some time to catch my breath. I drank some pineapple juice and lit a cigarette. In this spot giant hands—perhaps belonging to the same supernatural beings who built the pyramids of Egypt—have scooped out a huge triangle from the mountainside, forming a kind of terrace covered with low undergrowth but as level as a football pitch, with the cliff face as a backdrop. At the top of the cliff some large boulders protruded over the edge. I just hoped they were not planning to roll down on this of all nights. At the front of the terrace was my observation post: a hexagonal pillar of rock without the slightest irregularity that rose from the greenery below like a white bastion. At the top the pillar is hollowed out, creating a giant bathtub, whose rough walls look like the crenellated ramparts of a fortress. A natural stone bridge links the top of the column with the terrace. It had been from behind the fantastically shaped battlements of this fort that I had already observed the birds a couple of times without being seen by them.

Once I had recovered my breath a little, I shouldered the rucksack again, tore some branches off the shrubs and crawled on my hands and knees to my lookout post. Although the stone bridge is about eighteen inches wide and less than six feet long, crossing it is a scary business with the yawning abyss beneath you. But with the help of my guardian angel I reached the far side in one piece. Now I had to hurry, because it would soon be dark.

With the branches I had brought with me, I swept the bathtub as clean as I could. All kinds of vicious creatures could be hiding under the dry leaves and loose stones. I was particularly on my guard against scorpions. I get them in my own house occasionally, but they are the reddish-brown kind whose bite can sting and itch painfully, but which are otherwise harmless. However, their larger black relatives that live under stones and in withered cactuses are much more poisonous and can cause severe pain and fever. Country people say that you also develop a raging thirst, but that you mustn't drink any water, for then the poison will spread through your body and could be fatal. As a precaution I folded the bottom of my trousers tight around my legs and pulled my socks up over them. God knows what damage the poison glands of those diabolical creatures may do to certain body parts located below the belt. I took the blanket out of the briefcase and laid it down neatly folded in a corner of the fort so that it could serve as a seat for the time being.

Darkness fell quickly. The blue vault of the sky turned grey and the forest below was plunged into semidarkness; only on the highest treetops was there still a soft, silver glimmer that gradually faded. Near the summit of the mountain a young falcon hovered in its brown fledgling's plumage. The gaps between the bushes on the terrace opposite filled with ghostly silhouettes and mysterious blackness, and a dull red glow lit the steep cliff face. Then everything went dark and the wind got up. In the space of a few moments the setting sun took away all the beauty it had brought. The walls of the fort towered above me and I was sitting in the large square of darkness. I had my first shot of whisky.

Who could say how many slaves had met their deaths in the place where I was now sitting? The island's black population still tells strange stories about slaves who used to fly back to Africa. They still firmly believe that slaves who had eaten no salt were capable of this feat. The slaves sought out a high place, raised their arms to heaven, and took off on their flight to another continent. I can't believe that, even three or four hundred years ago, people were stupid enough to think that. But if the stories do have any basis in truth, this spot must have been an ideal takeoff point.

From a military point of view too, the place clearly had strategic importance. Were this island to be invaded—by Venezuela or Cuba, for example—and were the defenders of the town obliged to retreat from superior forces, they could withdraw to this high ground. The troops could camp on the terrace and five or six marksmen could position themselves in this natural fort. The fantastically shaped battlements would not only provide cover from enemy guns, but also enable the defenders to return fire unseen and hold out for a long time against their besiegers, who would be forced to clamber up towards them.

Later that evening the legions of mosquitoes moved into action — annoying little creatures that tried with all their might to get into my nose, ears and eyes. This aggression forced me to light up another cigarette and have a stiff drink. Alcohol, so beneficial and effective against so many things in this world, might also repel insects. In this spot the silence was even more oppressive than on my terrace. But here too the nocturnal darkness that had by now washed over everything had its own sounds: the wind through the trees and around the rocks, the rustling in the undergrowth, the dull thud of a stone dislodged from the cliff face, the unrecognisable call of an animal — sounds that in some mysterious way finally seemed to convey the same message of comfort.

I must have dozed off, because I suddenly awoke with a start as a sharp gust of air struck my face, as if some heavy shape had sped past, narrowly missing me. I recovered from my fright when I saw a large owl glide silently over my lookout post a few times and then swoop down to a rocky niche opposite. It perched upright in the aperture, its chalk-white underside clearly visible, looking like the statues of the Virgin you can see in Catholic shrines.

I had not sighted an owl for years. It is said they can see a hundred times more acutely than human beings, and that their hearing is so sensitive that even on the darkest night they can fly straight towards their prey, mostly mice and lizards, guided only by the tiny noises these creatures make. They swallow the mice and lizards whole and later regurgitate the hair and bones. Perhaps owls should be held up as an example to mankind. They mate for life and use the same nest year after year. There is another species of owl that is feared as a harbinger of death. It has a long, angular body resembling a coffin when it is in flight. If you see one of these, you must cross yourself quickly.

After some time, my white owl flew up out of the niche and, without a screech, disappeared into the night as abruptly as it had come. I decided that I might as well turn in. I spread the blanket out on the rocky ground, had a nightcap, and lay down.

The twentieth century was drawing to a close. I lay on my back and looked up at the silver disc in the sky. I am tall and skinny, so my feet touched the southernmost tip of Argentina and Chile, while my head lay against the coastal ranges of Venezuela. I spread my arms so that my left hand touched the Atlantic coast of Brazil and my right the Pacific seaboard of Peru. I stretched my arms above my head and my fingertips counted the Caribbean islands. It was dark over the whole continent and all the islands, and the darkness lasted the whole night.

In the hidden blackness of the *selvas* and on the pale, dun-coloured beaches, thousands of vague phantoms, the damned from five hundred years of Latin American history, emerge from their shadowy realm to torment the human beings of today, robbing them of their guns and jewels. The aerial roots of the mangrove forest lining the creeks waft their noxious breath over the landscape. Centuries-old trees, their branches malevolently twisted as if they wished to strangle all those who have been silently sinning for so long, wear a satanic leer in their weathered crowns—the grimace

of pain and impotence that cannot be erased because it is the suffering and helplessness of our ancestors. We are destined to feel its
consequences to our dying day, when we pass on the burden to our
firstborn son. Today's suffering is caused by what happened yesterday. For centuries a passive god has passed by the continent and the
islands in silence.

The torch of the sun that appears at dawn brings light but no
lightening of the load. This is the primeval sun created in the first
chapter of Genesis that surveys the entire continent and all the
islands, that knows everything because it can extract every secret
from the earth with its piercing light. It stores the gamut of human
experience in its fiery womb which, filled to the brim, boils, splits
and expels the charred excess in a blinding orgasm that astronomers
in Europe and the United States observe as the red excrescences of
the solar corona; but it continues uninterrupted on its orbit around
the world of men, uncovering new deeds and storing them in its
temporarily unburdened womb. The South American sun commits
a thousand murders every day, because it is not just the chronicler,
but also the instigator of the blackest human deeds. At six in the
morning it rises treacherously amid silver streamers that jubilantly
unfold, and at six in the evening it smothers itself in the yellowish-
red miasma of the swamp that fills the western sky.

In the false dawn of each new day, its first rays unravel the web
of the previous night and dispel the last of the morning dew's spar-
kling coolness. The continent and the islands awake and know that,
on this day like all the others, no one can escape the supremacy

of the sun. Knowing itself inviolable, the orb rises ever faster into the sky, embracing all things with its rampant heat. Struggling or resigned, human beings, animals, plants and all inanimate things reluctantly absorb the erectile sultriness. The higher the fireball climbs, the deeper, the deeper the heat penetrates into the gaping pores. Everything and everybody is infected and the carcinoma of heartless deeds can once again start to spread.

I woke up a few times during the night, partly because of the strange surroundings and the hard bed, but also because of the unpleasant thought that I might be stung by a scorpion or some other insect. At one point I tried to look at my wristwatch, but couldn't make out what time it was. I did not switch on the torch for fear of betraying my presence. Eventually I noticed that the night sky had taken on a lighter hue and from this I concluded that it would soon be daybreak. I folded the blanket neatly into a cushion I could sit on and took up my old position in a corner of the fort. I drank the rest of the pineapple juice and longed for a cigarette, but thought it better not to strike a match.

The dawn was longer coming than I had anticipated. Now and then I thought I could hear the creaking of a windmill, but it must have been something else, as I knew there were no windmills in this high country. It could have been the rattling of the ankle chains of a slave whose ghost, still bearing the scars of the floggings he had suffered, wandered endlessly through the night. This, at least, was how the country people explained such nocturnal noises. The Roman Catholic Church had been unable to expel completely the

African god brought from Angola and Calabar, unable to banish the invisible child-snatcher that roams the primeval darkness of the island, unable to suppress the illicit worship of saints.

Finally the sun broke through and the first misty light began to grope its way over the landscape, slowly revealing itself to the greenery and bare boulders in the valley. In the distance the birds flew up from their roosting places in the treetops and raised their coarse screeching to the heavens. High in the air they fell silent, grouped themselves into ragged V-formation and dived down in a swift parabola amid renewed cries. The flock flew upwards again, brushing the top of the cliff face, but I saw that at least two of the birds had not made it. In the place where they had crashed I saw a small crowd of feathers glistening in the sun, like the luminous green of an exploding firework.

I took a swig of whisky and lit a cigarette, greedily inhaling its smoke. It would be best not to tell anyone about this morning ritual of the birds. If it ever becomes widely known, people will come from far and wide to watch. The travel agents in town will advertise in the press, offering excursions to "the only place in the world where splendidly plumaged birds commit mass suicide in the light of the morning sun." The island authorities would apply for European development funding and use the money to convert the dilapidated private house on the other side of the mountain into a luxury restaurant with an exotic menu. The plateau next to me would be cleared of trees and undergrowth so that open pavilions thatched with palm leaves could be built for tourists to spend the night in. The natural bridge would be fitted with railings and the ramparts of the little fort protected with wire mesh to prevent the children who had been brought along to see the suicidal spectacle from falling off the mountain. The result of all this would, of course, be the rapid departure of the birds from the area.

The brief display was over and it was time to begin the descent and head home. I gathered up my things and stuffed them into the briefcase. I unwrapped the sandwiches and left them behind. Just as I was about to leave, a lizard appeared on the white wall. It was a tree lizard, more slightly built and darker than its relatives that scuttle along the ground. At first it watched me without moving, and then began to make agitated movements with its head. Finally it raised itself up and several times extended the brilliant blue and orange fold of skin under its throat like a fan. Some say that lizards do this when they feel threatened, others claim the male does it to attract the female. The boys of the island believe that if a lizard spreads its fan several times in succession it is insulting their mothers, and they promptly stone it to death.

THREE

The only tangible objects in the cocoon I have spun for myself are the glass on my left and the beer bottle on my right. The night is getting cooler. Half-transparent wisps of cloud float across the dark heavens and dim the brightness of the stars. I long for one of these mild shapes to descend upon the island, brushing my body with a consoling caress like a velvet-skinned woman, faintly perfumed and whispering soft words.

The night speaks to me. I listen to its sounds and try to decipher their message. I attempt to receive the faintest signals from those unfathomable depths of the universe where the darkness is eternal and the prehistory of all living matter lies hidden. I try to recall the history of everything that guides and influences me; whatever it is that persuades me to sit on my terrace at two in the morning and drink my life away. Sometimes I succeed in freeing myself for a moment from time and space, from attachment and shyness. Then the people and the dogs and the sins that have forced their way into my life disappear like impurities, and in that hallowed mood I am no longer at odds with my own being. The beer and the whisky, though both necessary to set the process in motion, become super-fluous at the point when the gaseous mixture mantling the earth changes composition and from the canopy of heaven a cool breeze of freedom and timelessness wafts towards me, containing ecstatic extracts of cactus, mushroom and ergot. A shiver runs through my limbs and it is as if the weight of my melancholy and the threat of the future are shaken from me. My sense of balance deserts me and I am overcome by a dizziness which creates the illusion that depths, emptiness and old fears can be erased, that happiness can simply be conjured up.

I have felt this dizziness at longer or shorter intervals throughout my life, sometimes at very inconvenient moments when I did not know how to respond. I found the sensation particularly annoying when I was young, and felt awkward enough anyway. It is only recently that I have begun to summon up the feeling deliberately; I call it my "solitary game."

As far as I can remember, I was about eleven or twelve when I first experienced this vertigo. It happened at school, but luckily I was alone at the time. As a boy I went to a Catholic school, simply because it was the nearest one to my home. The Protestant school was in a different part of town and to reach it you had to cross the big pontoon bridge, so my parents thought it safer to send me to the nearby Catholic school. Each day began with half an hour's religious instruction, with the emphasis on the Seven Sacraments and the Ten Commandments, which were relentlessly and repeatedly analysed. As a non-Catholic I did not take part in these catechism classes, and so in each term's report, alongside the words "Religious Instruction," there was always an oblique stroke rather than a mark out of ten. For the first half-hour of each day I sat with a textbook open in front of me, but did not read it because I was secretly following the lesson. I did so because those classes taught me something about what was happening within me and outside me, neither of which I fully understood.

Two or three times a year, on Catholic feast days, an open-air mass was celebrated in the playground. Everything had to be prepared the day before. The sections of the prefabricated wooden altar were taken out and assembled; a rectangular red carpet was laid out in front of the altar and tubs of flowers were placed on either side. The large space beyond the altar was filled with an enormous number of benches, which the boys had lugged out of the dining hall and corridors and placed in two dead-straight lines. The previous afternoon the whole school had marched in procession to the church to confess, so that they could take communion during the open-air mass. While this was happening, I stayed behind at school and hung about. There was also a Jewish boy from a higher class, but I paid no attention to him.

And the following day too, when all the boys and the priests were attending mass, I was left to my own devices. Though I was supposed to stay in the classroom and go over the day's lessons, I didn't feel much like doing so. My classroom was on the second floor and, tucked safely away behind a row of flower tubs in the corridor, I watched events down in the playground with interest and a mixture of feelings. It struck me as some weird kind of play being performed in an incomprehensible language, but at the same time I was attracted by the mysterious gestures of the priest before the altar, by the Latin words that he would sometimes mutter inaudibly and at other times sing out at the top of his voice, by the swinging of the censer and the tinkling of the little bell.

It was now time for the boys to take communion. They left their benches and lined up by classes before the altar, their teachers in front. When it was the turn of my class, I left my hiding place, went into the classroom and made straight for the cupboard where equipment was stored, as I knew it contained a telescope. It was right at the top and I had to stand on the bottom shelf to reach it.

The telescope belonged to the teacher. He had once taken the instrument to pieces, explaining to us in detail how it worked. Then he allowed each of us in turn to look out of the window through it for a few seconds. The teacher used the telescope for bird watching, which was, he said, a fascinating hobby. He often told us delightful stories about how birds behave, invariably concluding by making a comparison with human beings. In the garden behind the school there was an upturned metal drum on which every day the teacher would put out a bowl of water, bread crumbs and some sugar for the birds. He would position himself some distance away, half-hidden, and observe the creatures through his telescope. We had once been allowed to walk in the garden during breaks, but ever since one of the boys from the senior classes emptied an inkwell into the rain gauge set up there, and no one would name the culprit, the garden was off-limits to all pupils.

For some reason, one of the teacher's stories has stayed with me. It was about a pair of troupials that came to eat and drink at exactly the same time every afternoon. They were beautiful specimens, with their sharply contrasting deep-orange and gleaming black feathers.

One day the pair arrived with two chicks, which, in contrast to their parents, were bald and grey. With the exception of baby chickens, the friar told us, all young birds are ugly. These chicks had gaping beaks, and their parents fed them first, before eating anything themselves. The funny thing was that after a week or so, when the little ones had learned how to feed and threw themselves greedily on the food on the drum, they were pecked and driven off by their parents. Only after Mum and Dad had finished their meal were the little whippersnappers allowed at table. The friar concluded his story with a short sermon about parental wisdom and love, and about the respect and gratitude that all boys owed to their father and mother.

Armed with the telescope, I went back into the corridor, crouched behind the tub and followed the activities in the playground, now at very close quarters. In one hand the priest held a large chalice that looked as if it were made of gold and with the other hand he distributed the wafers. He had long, elegant fingers—I could even make out his well-manicured nails. A boy from my class took a couple of timid steps forward, with a look of something like alarm on his face. He knelt down rather stiffly in front of the priest, who carefully placed the wafer on the boy's pink tongue. I saw the boy's expression brighten immediately and I was glad, although I did not know why. Then I suddenly felt an emptiness in my head and sweat forced its way out of every pore in my body. I became paralysed, as if all my soft tissue had lost its resilience and all my bones had become petrified. With one hand I clung to the edge of the tub, and with the other I pressed the telescope desperately to my chest so as not to drop it. I thought I had suddenly been taken ill, and was terrified. But I was not ill, because the fear in my heart soon gave way to a strange feeling of relief, which was replaced in turn by an intense happiness that seemed to fill not only my body but the whole corridor.

My second dizzy spell occurred under very different circumstances more than a year later, during the summer holidays. I was staying with an aunt and uncle who lived out of town in a mansion, but because they were rather elderly, I spent most of the day on Tochi's little farm not far away.

Tochi and his wife were both warm, cheerful people who didn't give a damn about the sordid aspects of life and seldom took anything seriously. They were very similar in appearance as well: both were short, fat and rotund, and both had broad, dark-brown faces that were always gleaming. They had a daughter and two sons, the youngest of whom, Cinto, was my age.

Tochi grew a variety of vegetables and usually managed to sell all his produce to the big tourist hotel on the coast. But his crops often failed, either because they were attacked by insects and other vermin or because the rain stayed away for too long and the well dried up. This inspired the crafty Tochi to involve himself more directly with the island's tourist industry. The sandy track that ran past his farm to the coast had once been the only link between the hotel and the main road to town. The track wound its way along the foot of the Montenegro, a range of quite steep hills that reached almost to the coast and was quite dangerous because stones and boulders sometimes rolled down the slopes. At one time the track had been lined with signs in English warning the tourists of falling rocks, but these were soon removed by the locals for firewood. When a second modern hotel was built on the coast, a four-lane asphalt road was constructed on the other side of the hills as a direct link with the town and the airport. The new road was considerably longer, so many economy-minded American tourists continued to drive along the sandy track, especially as the tourist brochures described it as a "scenic route." This gave Tochi the idea of exploiting the holiday market. A short distance from his house he kept three large boulders ready at the side of the track, and in lean times he would roll them onto the roadway with a thick pole so that cars could not get past. It was Cinto's job to hang around nearby until a car carrying tourists, usually a man accompanied by a scantily dressed woman, came along and pulled up at the road block. The man would usually get out and try to shift the massive stones. At that moment Cinto would arrive and offer in broken English to call his father and big brother, who would be able to roll the boulders out of the way. The offer would be eagerly accepted. At the beginning Tochi charged five dollars for this service, but since the day when a tourist had pressed ten dollars into his hand he had changed his tactics. Now, when he and his sons had cleared the road and the tourist asked how much he owed him, Tochi would say, "I may be a poor farmer with a family of twelve to support, but if a man helps a fellow human being, he mustn't charge money for it." This almost always resulted in the tourist slipping little Cinto a ten-dollar note. An elderly couple once even gave them twenty-five dollars. Every time they pulled off this con trick, Tochi would say to his sons, "We'll go on doing this until we get our fingers burned. But why should they catch us out? We don't do it every day, and those tourists only stay a few days at the hotel and others come in their place. We can't live on air."

I heard the whole story from Cinto, with whom I also used to go and spy on Shon Joshi. These spying missions were exciting in themselves, because they meant running the gauntlet of the ferocious-looking dogs that guarded the property, but I could never see what was so special about Shon Joshi. Cinto was full of enthusiasm, though: "You must go and see the old guy. Everyone for miles around knows him and hates him, but has great respect for him. He's got a huge prick and he uses it every day. He's rich. He's been to bed with almost every girl around here. My father once said that if he ever laid a finger on my sister Rosamaría, he'd chop him into a hundred pieces with his machete. And the randy goat is really old. He's over sixty! But he's got a super-prick, because he drinks turkey blood every morning. Hot blood, straight from the bird's neck. He must have a thousand turkeys. You really must see the horny old slob."

Shon Joshi lived in a splendid white mansion with a massive roof, a number of elegant dormer windows, and a raised front terrace flanked by corner turrets. He had a big turkey farm and every year at Thanksgiving and Christmas he slaughtered hundreds of birds and sold them to the tourist hotels.

We climbed over the fence and crept stealthily through the undergrowth. "It takes longer from this direction," explained Cinto, "but it's safer. If you walk into the wind the dogs can't catch your scent, and if we don't make any noise they won't notice us." We crept behind the long row of cages. It was the first time I had seen live turkeys. I thought they were hideous, with their swollen combs and wattles and their dreadful high-pitched squawks. When we got closer to the house, we looked for a well-camouflaged spot from which to survey the terrace and wait until Shon Joshi emerged. "He's got at least ten or twelve maids," said Cinto, "all of them sixteen or younger. The men who feed the turkeys and clean out the cages are never allowed in the house, and if they trespass they're sacked and kicked out. Look, there he is!"

I had expected a giant of a man, an imposing figure bulging with muscles, but Shon Joshi turned out to be a short, puny creature, dressed in an immaculate tropical suit that seemed too big for him. On his neck I could see red combs and wattles, smaller versions of the ones on his turkeys, and there were brown lumps on his cheeks and forehead. He walked up and down the terrace a few times with a cautious, mincing gait, then looked up at the hot sun, took out a white handkerchief, wiped the backs of his hands with it and quickly disappeared back into the house. "Come on, let's get out of here," whispered Cinto almost triumphantly.

"My leg's gone to sleep, I can't get up yet," I lied. "I'll come along in a minute."

This was because at that moment I felt the strange dizziness in my head. I was now in the house following Shon Joshi down a long passage. He was no longer the seedy little man I had seen a few minutes earlier, but a handsome eastern prince, complete with moustache and short beard. When he reached the end of the passage he opened a heavy oak door with a bold gesture and strode through. From the room beyond wafted a pungent, pleasant perfume that I inhaled deeply. I too was an Arabian prince, clad in a colourful costume with sleeves that were much too wide and wearing a wine-red turban secured by a golden clasp on my head. As I stood in the doorway, I was obliged to give my eyes time to adjust to the semi-darkness. Although there was an enormous chandelier with at least a hundred slender branches hanging from the ceiling, none of its lamps gave more light than a candle. I was in a very large chamber, whose four walls were hung with patterned curtains and rugs with scenes woven into them that made me blush. The floor was strewn with huge, plump cushions, and I blushed even more when I saw the scantily clad young women sitting or lying on the cushions in shameless poses. But I plucked up my courage and, ignoring the leers of the sprawling girls, marched determinedly between the cushions to the back of the room.

There sat Rosamaría, Cinto's sister, who was four years older than him. She had constructed for herself a kind of armchair out of salmon-pink cushions and she half-lay and half-sat upon it, in exactly the same position I had seen her in that morning, in a hammock on the small terrace in front of her parents' house. At the time she had looked at me with troubled but kind eyes, and I even thought I saw a faint smile on her lips. Now she was sitting with her face to the wall, and I concluded from this that she was desperate to keep apart from the other girls. I stood behind her, leant forward a little and saw through the semitransparent fabric that swathed the outlines of her mysterious brown body. Embarrassed, I stepped back and lowered my eyes, but immediately afterwards I took another look. I stretched out my right arm and softly stroked her cheek with the backs of my fingers. I hoped she wouldn't notice the slight trembling of my hand, and would not turn round and look me straight in the eye. But she remained motionless and I continued to stroke her cheek. Then I touched her ear with my fingertips and ran my thumb along one of her eyebrows a few times. Like that morning, I thought I saw a faint smile on her lips and felt embarrassed and gratified at the same time. Then she leant back further and pressed her head against my chest, which gave me a pleasant tingling sensation.

Outside, the gobbling of the turkeys and the barking of the dogs ceased, and in the sudden silence I was able to distinguish tiny noises. I was still crouching in the same spot in the undergrowth. There was the faint hum of insects in the warm afternoon air, and a smell of dry soil and dead leaves. From the top of a tree came the hesitant cheep of a young bird, fresh from the nest, trying out its voice. A few large yellow leaves, their work done, came spiralling down to cover the nakedness of the forest floor. Close to where I was sitting, a large bush and a dark red vine clung together in a passionate embrace.

It was the first time I had an erection thinking about a girl.

FOUR

Under the influence of drink, I can look at an animal, a plant or a stone with a child's eye and suddenly see everything anew, hoping in my befuddled way for a miraculous release that will allow me to start life again with a clean slate. Sometimes alcohol disperses the demons of the night, soothing the exhausting tensions inside me and healing my seared mind, heart and conscience. Unerring as a laser, a healing ray of light falls from the moon's silver sickle onto my path.

Drink the great healer; the treacherous quack. I'm well aware, even when drunk, that what I'm so eager to clasp to my bosom may be no more than a temporary illusion. An adult can never become free again—he can never shake off the impure things that have attached themselves to his life with their suckers. There is no way back. But I drink, and in my brief intoxication allow myself to be carried back to a period when my life was not yet withered. Otherwise I should have to content myself with the implausibly calm existence of a naïve old man who thinks he should be happy because no great catastrophes have befallen him.

And yet, just as a boy in the process of becoming a man doesn't know what to do with his arms and legs, which have suddenly grown longer and collide clumsily with doorways, so the adult looking back at his youth staggers under the weight of years. When you are no longer young, everything pristine and untainted is a reminder of death. That's when my solitary game becomes dangerous.

I sit on my terrace and command the ridges of the hills to stop their grotesque metamorphoses. I order the exotic night birds to cease their hysterical cries. The world becomes silent and motionless, and I try to summon up that dizziness in my head which takes me back to childhood. But the great arch of the sky buckles, the starless heavens have come noiselessly off their hinges and begin to collapse, slowly at first, then faster as if trying to suffocate me. The air becomes compressed between heaven and earth. I'm lying on a hard bed gasping for breath. The pure dream that had begun to emerge disintegrates and I feel a burning fever all over and unbearable pain in my limbs. My eyelids are swollen and my eyes sting. When I half-open them, I'm looking into the ugly features of the *curandera*, who is leaning over the bed stuffing herbs under my pillow. Then she goes to the foot of the bed and starts smearing a black paste on the soles of my feet.

The moon wind blew for the first time around the middle of the seventeenth century when, by the light of a full moon, the itinerant priest Plácido died a martyr's death on a limestone plateau on the north coast, slain by a drunken, red-haired mercenary. Ever since, the phenomenon has been repeated in the same place almost every September. There has not been a single family from the village lying at the foot of the plateau that has not had at least one member snatched away by the terrible moon wind and the raging fever it brings. The three shops in the village sell only sombre mourning garb, as no one ever has a chance to don colourful clothes; before the two years of mourning for one victim are up, there is always a new death in the family. No one plays music in their houses or even in the village's two bars. The men and women wear such surly expressions, and even the children are serious when they play. The late poet Pierre L. once read me a moving poem, an epic without a hero, in which he calls the village successively Village of Mourning, Village without Music and Village without Smiles.

Legend has it that, when Father Plácido's strength was failing and he sank, mortally wounded, onto the chalky ground, purple blood flowed from his Spanish body. There came a roar like that of a gale, but the brightly lit night was windless and the atmosphere was sultry. The rumbling in the sky persisted. It was a sound that the soldiers had never heard before, and it filled them with a strange fear. The heat became almost unbearable, and all the air seemed to be sucked away. Cursing, the soldiers unbuttoned their tunics, revealing sweaty, hairless chests that glistened in the moonlight. Suddenly an icy blast came whistling across the plateau and chilled them to the bone. They took refuge in a cave, but the moon wind fever was already coursing through their bodies. None of them left the cave alive. The eleven skeletons were found some twenty-five years later.

Each September, when the moon is full, the villagers gaze into the sky with resignation on their faces but bitterness in their hearts. If they see a purplish glow around the lunar disc, they know the moon wind is on its way. They quickly lock themselves in their houses. Everything is shut tight; they stuff folded newspapers and strips of rag between the closed shutters and in every chink, so that not a breath of air can get in. When the wind has gone from the plain and the heat returns, it becomes boiling hot inside the houses, but people know that they are safe from the biting cold that will roar past. But almost every year there are victims. A window swings open in a little room where a baby is crying because of the heat. An old man, ignorant of the danger, sleeps off his hangover behind the tavern. A rash youth refuses to give credit to a silly legend.

When rumours started to circulate that the island's Catholic authorities had begun an inquiry into the life and death of Father Plácido, with the object of starting the official process of canonisation, or at least beatification, some of the villagers saw this as an excellent opportunity to gain favour with the saint-to-be and thus stop the moon wind. They organised a collection with the aim of erecting a statue of Father Plácido. There was a shady Italian in town with a flourishing trade in magic potions, designed to protect you against evil influence, bind a loved one to you forever, cause children's milk teeth to come through painlessly and much else besides; hearing of the collection, the Italian announced that he was in fact a trained sculptor and would be glad to offer his services. As a sample of his work he produced a painting showing a rather stocky man with his face raised piously to heaven and his habit half-open to reveal a snow-white chest bearing a purple heart; "The Violet Saint," read the inscription. But the statue never materialised, because the rumours about canonisation were false. The diocese found it necessary to issue a communiqué containing the startling revelation that neither the Archivo General de Indias in Seville nor the archive of the apostolic prefecture in Caracas contained any information about a Father Plácido.

Thus the Violet Saint remained unpropitiated and the moon wind still sweeps across the plain almost every year. Men, beasts and plants alike are affected when, in the midst of scorching heat, the freezing wind unexpectedly descends from the mountains and chills everything in its path. Young vegetables lose their sheen and come out in black spots, tamarind husks shrivel on the branch and unripe mangoes and medlars fall from the trees, riddled with tiny grey worms. The morning after the full moon, cattle are found with paralysed hind quarters. Pregnant goats lie on their backs and writhe in pain as violent abdominal cramps choke the young inside them. Not a single offspring of any species survives exposure to the moon wind. Small children lose all power of movement, their skin develops thick, ugly folds and death follows swiftly; older children may hold out for two or three days, but very few withstand the devastating fever. In grown men and women it lasts from eight to ten days. With eyes tight shut, distorted mouth agape and cheeks seemingly turned to leather, the victims lie in bed with trembling limbs, constantly shifting from their left side to their right. Their families and neighbours busy themselves day and night administering folk remedies that are supposed to draw the fever from the head of the sufferer to the soles of his feet, so as to quench the heat ravaging his body. After a week, sometimes a little longer, the patient suddenly rolls over onto his back, his arms and legs stop trembling, his glazed eyes are half-open and his tanned face begins to look like a death's head. The priest is hurriedly summoned to give the last rites with professional aplomb.

Occasionally some man or woman who is stronger in body, mind and faith survives the fever, but no one escapes the chastisement of the Violet Saint without some memento. Pipi Gatiero, the skinny village drunk who no one thought would recover, was left with a permanently bent neck, so that his head lolls ridiculously when he walks. "The booze in my blood was my salvation," he constantly intones, and drinks more than ever. Since his miraculous recovery Fèfè Notisiero has had ten stiff fingers that he cannot persuade to move. All day long he sits on his step violently shaking his head. His grandson sits next to him, and from time to time shoves a pipe into the mouth of the old man, who sucks furiously on it. Since Fèfè used to be a keen domino player and now walks around with his fingers splayed, the village boys have nicknamed him "Double Five." Chela, the only loose woman in the village and one of the few females to have withstood the fever, emerged from her ordeal without a hair on her head. For years she wore a black headscarf day and night, but now she goes around in a luxuriant wig. Tough old Don Bèni, who owns more goats than anyone else, escaped with nothing more than slurred speech. This was because his wife summoned a doctor from town who gave him injections. In his case the fever lasted only six days. "I have lived twice," Don Bèni never tires of telling anyone who will listen. "In those days of delirium my whole life—even things I had long forgotten—passed before my mind's eye in the minutest detail. I have lived twice, and the second time around every experience was more intense."

Each time someone survives the moon wind sickness, their feverish hallucinations are the talk of the village. There is also some interest in the capital: a few years ago a learned researcher wrote a thesis entitled *A Psychological Study of the Experiences of Nine Survivors of Moon Wind Fever*, which provoked much controversy. A civil servant from the government medical service even appeared on television to dismiss the so-called moon wind fever as nothing more than a severe form of dengue.

The survivors are unanimous in stating that, throughout the whole time the fever rages, any kind of restful sleep is impossible, and that this leads to utter mental and physical exhaustion; this must be why so few people recover. There are lucid moments when the patient observes everything around him with burning eyes — but he is so exhausted that he can do nothing, and eventually his consciousness clouds over again and he drifts into a half-waking state where he can hear voices and other sounds but cannot identify them. He is overwhelmed by terror as he feels himself sinking further into the morass of his fading consciousness. He thrashes about in a futile attempt to escape the swampy blackness engulfing him.

"He's trying to talk, praise be to the Mother of God," echoes another voice. "O Queen of heaven, hear the plea of Thy black slave and drive out the fever from the body of this man. Blessed be the name of Thy Son."

Try as I may, I keep drifting into a new delirious dream. I hear the voices of black women, I see white women's breasts with firm, reddish-brown nipples: an incoherent dream full of squirming, slippery creatures, lisping sounds and warm orifices. My body trembles, possessed by a strange exultation, and I try to sit up, but I am forcefully thrust back into a prone position to continue my rhythmic contortions on the bed. Over the pitch-black pool I find myself in,

a faint greyish glow begins to break. A shadow comes to life, a shape-
less mass that writhes slowly forward, now swelling to a terrifying
bulk, now shrinking to a thin ribbon, then growing once more into
a strapping giant with a thousand arms that wave like the tentacles
of a polyp. I hear a shot and wake with a start, paralysed by fear. I
don't know whether the shot was in my dream, or whether someone
actually fired a gun nearby. Or did I fire the shot myself? Did I reach
out and take the pistol off my bedside table? Birds die in the blue of
morning too, I say to myself, without knowing why.

It is not completely dark in the room I am in, as there is a small
fire burning somewhere. I cannot make the fire out itself. But I can
see the flickering of its flames reflected on the massive roof beam
above my head. The only sound I can hear is the guttural rattle I
produce as I inhale the cold air through my nostrils and expel it
feverishly, causing a dull pain in my chest. Where did the chatter-
ing women go? It's probably the middle of the night and everyone is
asleep. But it's nothing new for me to be lying alone at night while
other people sleep. Once again I am lying, as I used to, in the little
square of dark.

But I am not alone. Someone is sitting at the foot of my bed. One
of the old women? What has she brought now? Another bowl of
iguana soup to build up my strength, or another infusion of lemon
grass that she will make me drink while it's still boiling so as to drive
out the fever? I cannot identify the nodding figure.

"Are you awake?" I recognise the old woman's voice.

"What? I don't know . . ."

"It's best not to talk, it'll tire you out. You must save all your strength to get better. *Santísima Virgen,* make this son's body healthy again. Is there anything this old woman can do for you? Do you want a drink?"

"I need a pee."

"Oh, that's easy. I'll just get the can."

The blanket is shoved aside and with strong hands the woman rolls me onto my right side.

"Have I got my trousers on?"

"Yes, just a minute, we're almost there."

The callused hands fiddle roughly with my body. Then she says, "It's hanging in the can. Go ahead."

As the burning liquid leaves my body I experience enormous relief. Then I feel myself sinking back into the blackness of a yawning chasm. The last thing I hear is the splash as the old woman throws the contents of the can out through the doorway.

The grey fronds before my eyes turn into the green of a papaya plantation. I see endless, dead-straight lines of trees, their six-fingered leaves waving in the wind, and I begin to hope that the breeze they are sending in my direction will dispel all the pain. I look up at the white clouds gliding mysteriously past against the vast blue backdrop. The shadows are dark on the earth, but white in the sky. These clouds are the white shadows of things on the earth, the capricious silhouettes of mountains, trees, houses and people driven silently and aimlessly across the sky like insubstantial veils and fleshless forms. The spectacle does not last long. Low on the horizon a broad grey band spreads and in the far distance there is the dull, intermittent rumble of thunder. The white clouds and the blue backdrop darken and draw a new, hazy night over themselves. Everything goes black.

The next night—in my delirium, that is—I am a boy of about eleven. I am staying with my uncle, who lives on the mainland, and am lying on my back on the roof of the house. I am watching incredibly large white clouds being blown into each other by the wind, like fragile curtains, and finally being driven away to distant countries. The corrugations of the iron roof are hurting my back, but I do not move. Any movement would make the metal creak and betray my presence. And anyway I welcome the pain. I lie there motionless.

The evening dew makes the metal sheets freezing cold, and the soreness in my back is almost unbearable. I clench my teeth and squeeze my eyes tight shut. Perhaps the pain will get so bad that I will die. In the morning, when the sun rises and the roof begins to warm up, I shall be dead: a corpse with eyes tight shut and clenched teeth. The birds of prey that live in the mountains will discover my body during their early morning reconnaissance and start to circle the house. Suddenly they will hang perfectly still in midair, and if no one in town is watching them, they will swoop like lightning down onto the roof. They will rip my flesh, greedily drink my blood and crush my bones. When their bellies are full, they will fly off with the remaining scraps of meat and bone to feed their young in their nest high in the mountains. Then it will pour with rain, washing all trace of blood off the roof.

No one will know what has happened to me. In the eyes of my classmates at the Colegio Aquino, I shall be a hero: a schoolboy who simply vanished off the face of the earth! The old women in our neighbourhood will say that it is not the first time a boy on the threshold of manhood has been abducted by an evil spirit. He'll be lying at the edge of town somewhere, they'll say, in some dark place where people seldom go, foaming copiously at the mouth. The men will jeer at the women and say the boy has met a rich lady who has fallen in love with him and that he's now living like a lord in the capital. Who'd have thought it of such a well-behaved boy, brought up strictly and with a smile for everyone. My uncle the minister will call in the police to search for me, and if they find nothing he will send a sad telegram to my parents and probably pray for weeks for the return of the prodigal son.

I am lying not on a corrugated iron roof, but on a hard bed, and I have pains not only in my head, but also in my chest and throat. I am awake now, but I keep my eyes tight shut and my teeth clenched; I breathe laboriously through my nose. To judge by what I can hear, there are a lot of people in the room — men, women and children — and there is a lot of noise: the hubbub of the voices, the clatter of plates, pots and pans, and a scraping noise as if something is being dragged across the floor. I am surprised to find that, in spite of feeling pain all over, I feel at ease amid the turmoil of this strange room and among these people who are not part of my past. What am I doing here? Why am I not at home in my own bed? Is anyone missing me? Why am I not being rescued from this hole by my relatives?

"This one's on the way out," I hear a man's voice say. "That lousy Violet Saint of yours is already cheering in heaven."

"*Por Dios*, Bencho!" cries an alarmed woman's voice. "I wouldn't say things like that if I were you. It's just asking for trouble. You'd better cross yourself right away."

Suddenly there is complete silence, as if everyone has disappeared and left me alone in an empty room. A new dream is about to start. I can see no images, but I know that I am in a secluded spot in the forest, and I inhale the scent of thick undergrowth and newly dug earth. I open my eyes to see where I am, but I am back on the hard bed again, with two female figures moving about at the foot. I cannot make them out with any clarity, because the dream seems determined to stay incoherent. Then my delirium is completely dispelled by the sharp sunlight that streams through the doorway and casts a pattern of rectangles across the floor.

My eyes adjust to the light and I can at last see the two old witches. One of them is a real virago, tall and wide, with an enormous head of curly hair that glistens hideously from an excess of coconut oil and looks like a nest of young snakes. She is holding a dove in each hand, white creatures with red eyes incessantly jerking their heads back and forth. The second woman is equally tall, but is thin as a rake and flat-chested; she holds a knife between her teeth and is tying a grubby apron around her companion. When she has finished, she pulls the blanket off me and rolls up my trouser legs. She takes one of the doves from the other woman and in one rapid movement she twists its wings over its back and holds it belly up in the palm of her left hand. Her fingers grasp the bird's neck and tail, so that it can move only its legs. With her other hand she takes the knife out of her mouth and with one swift stroke slits the dove open from neck to tail. The bird makes no sound. With the same dexterity the woman presses the creature she has cut open against the sole of my foot.

"Quick, cut the other bird open," she snaps, handing the knife to the virago. The huge woman makes an incision in the second dove and presses it against my other sole. The blood of the birds feels tepid at first, but then becomes burning hot. Is it my imagination, or can I feel tiny, convulsive flutterings of intestines and bird claws against the soles of my feet? I begin to feel sick and try to pull my feet away, but the nausea is already giving way to a sensation that completely paralyses me. It is as if my body is emptying itself, as if my internal organs are relaxing in a series of minor spasms, as if all my pores are gaping to allow some slimy liquid to seep out of me. I feel as if my body is melting and I am sinking slowly into a substance that is neither solid nor liquid, but feels almost unbearably sensual and delicious. My every fibre is trembling with exaltation.

"*Koño!*" exclaims the woman who is tucking me in. "This fellow can't be all that ill. Just look at his trousers. He's come all over the place!"

I cannot make out all the words that a warm mouth is whispering close to my ear, but in the sweet murmurings I recognise the sounds I used to hear so often on hot afternoons when, with a woman's sticky body pressed against mine, I rocked gently in a hammock that made faint rattling sounds. Suddenly I'm plunged into the tender warmth of Irma-Luz.

I never really got used to a hammock. With such an unstable structure you must take great care over every movement you make, and consequently I tumbled out of it a few times. Irma-Luz's hammock was an enormous affair that stretched from wall to wall across her large room and was lavishly decorated with scores of ribbons and strings of beads in every conceivable colour. But the two rows of rattles at either end were the craziest idea of all. Irma-Luz had made them from hollowed-out gourds, which she had painted in bright colours and filled with pebbles from the beach. The slightest movement you made in the hammock caused stones to rattle. From the very start the constant noise got on my nerves. "Do you realise that that stupid rattling could make a man impotent in time?"

"On the contrary," Irma-Luz had replied with a laugh, "don't you know anything about psychology? You'll probably be so conditioned by all that rattle that you'll get an immediate hard-on whenever you hear the noise!"

On the afternoon of one of those sultry days in early May when a tepid, paralysing veil envelops the whole island, Irma-Luz and I were lying motionless in the hammock, our sweaty bodies pressed together. The primeval force that had taken us to the heights of ecstasy had subsided, the arousal and the passion had turned to satiety and exhaustion, and we lay so still that even the rattles at the head and foot of the hammock were silent.

This tender silence was suddenly shattered by the wailing of sirens and the screech of tyres, hideous sounds that went on and on, as if at least a hundred ambulances or police cars were chasing each other down the street.

"Sudden voices always make me jump," Irma-Luz whispered

without opening her eyes. I had already felt the shock go through her body.

"Perhaps World War Three has broken out," I joked.

"There must have been some terrible accident—so many sirens, there's no end to them. I must have a look out of the window."

The stones rattled furiously as she jumped out of the hammock, and I had to roll quickly towards the centre of it to avoid falling out. She half-opened the window and we both caught the smell of burning that drifted in. She covered her breasts with her hands and leant out of the window.

"There's a big fire. I can see a huge plume of smoke somewhere near the bridge. Wait a minute, there's fire on the other side of the harbour too."

I joined her at the window and we counted four fires. Down below, a truck full of soldiers roared past, preceded by two wailing police motorbikes. We closed the window to keep out the pungent smell of burning and switched on the radio. We listened to the news with mounting dismay. The newsreader was hard to follow, because at intervals he would break into a hysterical scream. The room filled with a stream of shocking reports: a mass march of striking workers in the centre of town; cars overturned and torched; vandalism and looting in supermarkets; a mob robbed of its senses by stolen liquor; bloody clashes between demonstrators and police; crowds, shootings, arson and looting; the sealing off of the town centre and the closure of the airport; a ban on assembly, a ban on the sale of alcoholic drinks, the imposition of a curfew . . .

"I'll get you something to eat," said Irma-Luz. "You'd better stay here tonight. With that pale Protestant mug of yours you'd probably get lynched if you stepped into the street."

I spent this day when so much changed, when my sleepy native isle was rudely deflowered by revolt, pain and blood, with a woman whose skin was soft and medlar-coloured in a hammock adorned with rattling gourds.

Later, after midnight, Irma Luz sat in the hammock once more; she had had a bath and was still naked. She dangled her legs over the side and pressed a tiny transistor radio to her ear. Now and then she relayed a news report. I knelt in front of the hammock and put my hands on her knees. I spread her thighs wide and pressed my head into her lap. I don't know if it had anything to do with the smell of burning that still hung in the room, but her pubic hair smelt of incense, the same odour I had smelt as a small boy when mass was celebrated on the playground of my primary school. I lifted my head and studied the folds of her genitalia at close range. I realised at the same time that from below a thousand demons, and from above a thousand gods, were looking back at me.

FIVE

I spent my tenth and most of my eleventh year—probably the period in your life when you see and hear most new things—on the mainland with my Venezuelan uncle. The man was neither Venezuelan nor even my real uncle, but I called him that because he lived on the mainland and was married to a Venezuelan woman. He was an odd character, but I guess he meant well. In the early years of the oil industry he had worked for Shell, but after spending some time among the oil tanks that mushroomed on the north side of the harbour he felt a vocation to become a minister. He went to Europe to study and returned a few years later, not as a Protestant minister, but as an evangelist belonging to some obscure sect obsessed with showing mankind the error of its ways and threatening hellfire and damnation. In between he found time to marry a beautiful Venezuelan woman, whose jet-black eyes and long, raven-black hair I can still recall. They lived on the mainland but visited the island, he as guest speaker to deliver fire-and-brimstone sermons in a tiny church on the other side of the harbour, she to buy a fresh supply of jewellery and other items and take them back illegally.

Not that the *señora*'s smuggling was particularly secretive. When she left she was usually weighed down: three or four necklaces round her neck, her wrists covered in bracelets, and rings on all her fingers except the thumbs, sometimes even two rings per finger. On one occasion when I went back with them during the holidays, I saw her nearly get caught when she arrived at Puerto Cabello. In addition to the usual huge quantity of jewellery, she was lugging an enormous bag bulging with top-quality American chewing tobacco. Suddenly she was accosted by a customs officer with a great deal of silver on his cap and epaulettes, a youngish fellow with a tiny but smartly groomed moustache: "Madam, your bag is very large and heavy." "That's my Venezuelan aunt behind bars," I thought to myself. But she raised her head proudly and said, "You look like a charming young man, but you don't seem to realise that a lady's handbag contains secrets no man must ever see." The man had a light-brown complexion, but I still noticed he was blushing. He nodded speechlessly and made a helpless gesture with his hands — and the contraband was allowed straight through. Less than two years later she was killed in a train crash.

The "uncle" and his wife were childless, and during a two-week holiday with them I made such a good impression that they wanted to adopt me. That was impossible, of course, but they did persuade my parents to let them borrow me for a time. The decisive factor was their promise that I would receive an excellent education. Not much came of my studies, however, as the schools were closed for most of that year. Quite apart from the normal holidays, there always seemed to be a revolution or rebellion in progress somewhere in the country. The initial response to this was invariably to close the schools. And when the situation returned to normal, reopening the schools was always the last thing the authorities thought of. All this was fine with me, but I thought it better not to write home about it. When I returned to the island after two years, I was put in the fifth class of my old primary school, but was demoted to the fourth class after three weeks because I was behind in just about every subject.

My Venezuelan uncle was obsessed with two things: the Bible and chess. Thanks to him I still know many passages from the Scriptures by heart, and I learned to play chess so well that if I was angry with him for some reason, I could usually beat him in fewer than thirty moves.

Every Saturday without fail my uncle would visit the prisoners incarcerated in the Castillo and bring them the Word of God. I was often made to accompany him so that I could see "the ugly side of life." During the fifteen-minute work breaks and the one-hour lunch period, he would read to the prisoners from the Bible and speak words of comfort to them, emphasising the forgiveness of sins and God's great love for all men, even for them, whatever they had done wrong. We had to get everything ready for the trip on Friday evening, as we left on the first bus at six the next morning. My uncle would take books, magazines, pamphlets, and miniature draughts and chess set with him, and I had to lug a basket containing fruit and those hard, round biscuits that were so popular at the time. At about eight the bus reached its terminus at the village of San Vicente. It was always a dusty drive, through little villages that all looked the same, and the bus would get fuller and fuller and noisier and noisier. From San Vicente we had almost an hour's walk down a narrow country road before we arrived at the Castillo, a large, ugly building that looked nothing like a castle. By this time the inmates were already hard at work in the fields surrounding the prison. Hundreds of sweating men, all stripped to the waist, were busy digging, breaking stones, pushing heavy wheelbarrows or driving juddering drills into the ground. Two concrete mixers made an earsplitting din that never seemed to stop. All around, on low mounds and boulders, stood the uniformed guards, short, fat men who constantly wiped the sweat from their brows. They had long, old-fashioned rifles, and a few carried pistols.

Then came the sudden shrill whistle that everyone had been waiting for. The prisoners dropped their tools where they stood, or let their wheelbarrows crash to the ground, and hastily sought out a shady spot. My uncle would then join one group or another, and while the men lay on the ground smoking cigarettes, or pissed in the bushes, or stared absently in front of them, apparently without hearing or seeing anything, he would talk to them about God. Sometimes he would also play a game of draughts with one of the older prisoners, and between moves he would continue to talk about the second coming of Christ.

I used to sit on a boulder next to a man who kept himself apart from the other prisoners. He was tall and terribly thin; his eyes were lifeless and he seldom spoke. After I had been sitting next to him for some time, he would sometimes say, "Hello, lad." I would answer, "Hello, sir," and push the basket towards him, but he never took anything from it. Without saying a word, he would quickly smoke two or even three cigarettes in succession. Then the whistle would go and he would silently stand up and rejoin his work gang.

My uncle would come and sit with me for the hour and a half

until the next break and teach me the finer points of chess. Now and then he would approach the guards, but did not like to do so because they had forbidden him to talk about religion. He was allowed to do that only to the prisoners, because they needed it. "We're going to heaven anyway," the guards would scoff.

When the whistle went for the next break, my uncle would hurry over to another group and the thin man would take up his usual position. Dutifully, I pushed the basket towards him yet again, though I realised he would never take anything. Many times I sat on the boulder next to that man and in all those months he said only a few words. Still, I think we communicated spiritually and I learned something from him, though I'm not quite sure what.

The thin man lit up a cigarette and inhaled deeply. He looked upwards and I followed his gaze. Far away in the taut blue sky a bird of prey soared upwards, its wings motionless. It rose higher and higher and became smaller and smaller, until it was no more than a tiny black cross floating up to heaven. I had to stop watching because my eyes were beginning to ache from the bright sunlight, but the man kept on staring at the bird. What's going on in his head at this moment, I wondered. I felt sorry for him because he was in prison and couldn't go home that evening as I could.

He now had a cigarette end between his lips and had placed his hands on his knees. He clenched his fists, and I saw that the taut skin of his hands was like the tanned hides of reptiles displayed in shops. I had the feeling that his clenched fists were not a sign of impotent rage; it was more as if he was trying to cling on to something. At any moment I expected him to sigh, "Oh, how wonderful everything could have been." But he said nothing. Finally he lowered his head, and without blinking focused his attention on a dwarf bush a few yards away. It was a plant with dull green, saw-edged leaves which gave off a scarcely perceptible heat, suggesting that the bush was burning in some mysterious way. Beyond it was a low hill that had been deeply quarried out by the prisoners, creating a cave into which the sunlight fell obliquely. I watched the man and saw that he had looked away from the bush and was now staring at the gash in the hillside. For the umpteenth time I was struck by his tormented eyes and wondered whether he had clairvoyant powers. I looked back at the cave. It was probably stifling hot in there; who knows, it may have been home to the ghosts of prisoners who had succumbed to the brutal prison regime. If I strained my eyes, perhaps I could see the same things as the man sitting next to me. Halfway between us and the cave the sunlight and the darkness merged, and at that spot a clearly perceptible haze rose from the ground, in which the blurred reflection of the bush shimmered. Once again, I hoped that the man would say something, but the whistle sounded and he got up and left. I felt disappointed and slightly intoxicated. My eyes were hurting, there was a cramp in my legs and I was stiff all over from having sat for too long. I hated the merciless sun and the sandy soil on my skin and in my clothes.

The signal for the lunch break was a cannon shot from the Castillo. The iron gates of the prison opened with a hideous grating sound and a decrepit pickup truck drove out, bringing the food for the prisoners and guards. My uncle and I were given a portion from a large aluminium dish, invariably a greasy stew of rice, meat, beans and bananas. I took only a few mouthfuls. I preferred one of the hard biscuits from the basket, although they always gave me hiccups.

In the afternoon everyone worked at half-speed. The sun burnt even fiercer and the heat became almost unbearable. The pickaxes went into the ground at longer intervals, the wagons were filled more slowly and the wheelbarrows were pushed even more languidly. The guards sat on the mounds and the sweat marks around the armpits of their shirts grew larger and larger. The only one who did not malinger was my uncle. He spoke just as fervently about Our Lord in the afternoons as in the mornings.

Towards sunset, when it was time to go, my uncle would discover yet again that the basket was still full, and would ask me reproachfully, "Why didn't you distribute the things among the prisoners?" But he never waited for an answer. He took the basket and hurried over to the prisoners already lined up waiting to be counted before marching back to the Castillo.

Once on our way home I asked my uncle about the thin man with the dead eyes and about what crime he had committed, and my uncle answered abruptly, "That's *El Verdugo*. He's driven by the forces of darkness. His soul is damned. You mustn't bother with him." This noncommittal reply only increased my sympathy for the man on the boulder.

After those trips to the Castillo I would lie in bed in the evening utterly exhausted, my back aching from all the sitting. Yet it took me some time to get to sleep. I would listen to the guitar music that drifted into my room almost every evening from the alleyway behind

our house. It was usually a sombre, monotonous melody unaccom-
panied by any singing, which I found strange, as most people who
play the guitar seem to feel that they have to sing as well. Between
the strumming I heard other sounds: the cannon shots from the
Castillo, the whistles of the guards, the sharp hissing sound when
the air compressor was switched off, the loud clang when the tail-
gate of the pickup was dropped, the ceaseless clatter of pickaxes on
the rocky ground, the rattling voice of my uncle, who could speak at
such lightning speed about God in the work area of the prison. And
once again I smelt the odours of the day: the freshly baked bread at
the bus stop in the mornings, the starch from my uncle's clothes as
he sat bolt upright beside me on the bus, the orange and pineapple
that rose from the basket, the reek of rum on the guards' breath as
they talked to my uncle, and most of all the smell of newly dug earth
and crushed blocks of stone. I also saw an unending succession of
images floating towards me: the curious grimaces my uncle made
when he talked to the prisoners; the sweating, trembling flesh of
the workers as they thrust their pneumatic drills into the earth; the
clouded eyes of the man who never spoke, the man my uncle had
called a "thug" and who exhaled cigarette smoke in spiralling wisps
that dissolved like question marks in the windless afternoon; the
long shadows of the convicts as they marched back to the Castillo
in the twilight. Then I would shut my eyes even tighter, trying also
to close my ears to all sound and to breathe as gently as possible: I
strained to keep my body still, avoiding even the slightest movement
and banishing all thoughts except those of falling asleep. It was on

an evening such as this, when it was already dark and deathly quiet, that my boy's hands discovered the taut hardness and the unfamiliar warmth in my loins. But then at once I heard my uncle speaking, in a voice more thunderous than the cannon of the Castillo, of the hellfire that awaited all sinners.

SIX

I was often left by myself during the twenty months I spent on the mainland. After lunch my uncle always went out to declaim biblical texts or to convene mysterious meetings in derelict houses. He did not return until the evening, sometimes very late. His wife was constantly travelling into the city or out into the countryside to sell her contraband to wealthy people and plantation owners. This was how she supported her husband. I was left at home with an elderly maid who left at four in the afternoon. Yet I did not feel abandoned. That was the time when I learned to love solitude and books. Even now I look back on the reclusive years of my youth with a certain fondness.

On the frequent days when there was no school, my uncle would sometimes teach me math, Spanish, biblical history and chess in the mornings. In the afternoons, when he had gone out, I secretly read the books in his bookcase. This wasn't too easy at the start, but soon Spanish ceased to present any great difficulty. With few exceptions they were religious books, and I could not always understand the difficult passages. Eventually, because I was reading so much about religion and matters of faith and how man should live, I developed an intense curiosity about the other side of the coin. I yearned for "bad" books—but I was to have a long wait. In the meantime, however, I indulged my own fantasies, creating characters that I made do things I myself had never done. These fantasies, which sometimes lasted for hours and to which I was constantly adding new episodes, gave me great satisfaction and at the same time a sense of sinfulness, a contradiction that I blamed on the empty, silent house. I lived in a no-man's-land seemingly equidistant from bad and good. The image of my uncle would loom up before me, dressed in immaculately pressed clothes, each hair on his head kept in its place by the green pomade that he rubbed in each morning, its musty smell still reminiscent of candles that had just been snuffed out. His starched clothes emphasised the tenseness in his body. At his side, his cool, calm, stately wife was always in her Sunday best. At such moments I felt sorry for my uncle and his wife; I almost hated them and longed to be home again.

Naturally, I did not spend the entire twenty months cooped up in the house like a monk. I had two friends at school whose houses I sometimes visited, and I also went for walks through the city. I went into the country a few times too: our ten-day visit to Chimbarí was particularly memorable.

That visit took place when rioting broke out in the city. It all started with a strike at the two government factories. The workers demanded a rise, put down their tools and took to the streets. There was turmoil all day long, but by the evening everyone was drunk and then the real pandemonium began. Fires were started in the streets. The police, now supported by the National Guard, carried out baton charges and arrested a hundred or so workers. Because the police station did not have enough cells, the prisoners were taken to the officers' club just outside town, where they spent the night under guard in the tennis courts. In the morning, the workers were released and marched back to town.

When I went to school that morning, I found the big barred gate locked. I strolled round for a while with some other boys before setting off back home. As we got to the market a long procession of workers was just passing. A few young men at the front were singing, but the market women who lined the street in small groups greeted them with jeers and shouts.

"There go the heroes! Did you get your rise?"

"Are you going to be paid for yesterday and today?"

"What's your family supposed to eat today? Shit?"

Some of the women started to clap rhythmically and shout "Left-right, left-right, left-right," as if soldiers were marching past. At the sight of one worker who was hobbling past on one leg with the aid of a crutch, someone started shouting "Left-left," which was quickly taken up by the others.

That evening the *alcalde*'s house was stoned, one of the factories was burnt to the ground and a policeman was stabbed to death. The strike had turned into a riot.

My uncle considered it advisable to leave town until things had calmed down, so the following morning the three of us left for Chimbarí, where a good friend of his had a small farm. This was the first time I had ever been on a train and I thought it was wonderful, although I didn't like the noise it made or the soot from the locomotive that found its way into the carriages. I was wide-eyed with wonder. While my uncle sat bolt upright in his seat holding an open book far too close to his nose, and his wife sat like a bored queen on her throne cooling herself with an ivory fan, I gazed in fascination at the landscape passing by. At the start it was not particularly interesting, as the train was travelling through an arid region, but suddenly, without any noticeable transition, everything became green. I saw hundreds of tree-covered hills dotted with bright red cottages. How could families live in such remote, inaccessible places, I wondered. What did they do all day? What happens if someone is taken seriously ill? I saw huge mountains, some half-covered in dark green but with bare, grey summits, through which flowed a vast river, apparently scarcely moving. I saw green fields stretching to the horizon, grazed by enormous herds of cattle. Sometimes it seemed as if the train was cutting straight through the middle of a herd.

Chimbarí turned out to be no more than a small village with a few hundred inhabitants. But I was impressed by several large and elegant though run-down buildings and by a magnificent church, a lofty structure with two square towers that reminded me of a medieval castle. Its thick walls had cracks in them caused by earthquakes. My uncle told me that Chimbarí had once been a prosperous little town, the seat of a Roman Catholic bishop, and that the church dated from the Spanish period. As we looked at it in the glow of dusk, the church seemed to be surrounded by a halo of dying light. My uncle called it "a temple of God that has withstood revolutions, earthquakes and the confessed sins of many generations." The following morning we drove in an open carriage drawn by two horses to Sandoval's farm, which was just outside the village.

Like most of his countrymen, Sandoval was short of stature, and he constantly wriggled his shoulders as though his shirt were uncomfortable. He had a big head and a broad, puffy face; his fore-head and the loose, flabby skin on his cheeks shone as if they were coated with oil. Perhaps his head looked big only because he was so squat and had almost no chin. He was a very friendly man and I took to him immediately. His farm wasn't that small. The spacious house was surrounded on three sides by a veranda, so that it was always cool inside. He had about twenty cows and more than two hundred goats. Everywhere there was a fresh and distinctive smell that was very different from the city.

I went for long walks in the surrounding countryside and spotted many plants, trees and birds I had never seen before. I often went into Chimbarí, where I got the impression that no one worked, because everywhere in the village there were groups of men sitting in front of houses, under trees or in the bar. Once I went into the church with a boy from the village to see the carved wooden Madonna on a side altar, the Madonna of the Sad Face, whose eyes sometimes filled with tears that rolled down her cheeks and dropped onto an oak plank that had been attached to the base of the altar. The inside of the church was quite bare, the Madonna was not beautiful and I couldn't see any tears. The statue was in the habit of weeping during Lent, the boy told me, and at that time visitors often came from the towns to look at the Holy Virgin, to buy a candle and to light it on the little altar while praying for her intercession. Only a few of them had been fortunate enough to see the Madonna weep-ing, he added, but the stains of the fallen tears were clearly visible at the foot of the statue.

One afternoon I went into the bar for a glass of coconut milk. The place was packed and every so often the crowd of customers would howl or start applauding. Five men were playing a game that was being enthusiastically followed by everyone present, accompanied by a lively commentary. After watching intently for at least a quarter of an hour I still had no idea what was going on. It took a whole hour and an explanation by two strapping youths for me finally to understand, but even then I found it a silly game because none of the players wins or loses.

The game was called simply "date stones." Four men played, plus a questioner. The questioner was always the same person, a tiny, shrivelled old man who puffed constantly on a pipe that emitted clouds of evil-smelling smoke. He had a high-pitched voice like that of a toddler. I thought that was odd: a centenarian with the voice of an infant. He asked questions that had to be answered by the players in turn. At the start of the game the old dodderer had twenty-one dried date stones clutched in his right hand. If his question was answered correctly, he would lean forward and drop a date stone into the respondent's breast pocket. If someone did not know the answer or answered incorrectly, the same question was put to the other three players. If they did not know the answer, no one got a stone. In that case the old boy would turn to the audience, and if none of the spectators could answer either, he would beam with satisfaction and give the solution in vivid detail. If the spectators did know the answer, he would look sheepish and go quickly on to a new brainteaser. The old man went on asking questions until all the players had answered five correctly. Then he stood up rather defiantly, stretched out his arm and unclenched his fist to show everyone that there was nothing in his hand. Where was the twenty-first stone? That was what the game was all about and now the betting began. What had the old rascal done during the questioning? On an occasion when a player had answered correctly, he had slipped not one but two date stones into the man's pocket. He was therefore the only one who knew which player had six stones in his pocket at the end of the game. All the bystanders then bet amongst themselves for drinks, cigarettes or money. Each punter chose two of the four players in the game. When all the bets had been laid, the old man gave the signal and the four players emptied their pockets. An earsplitting roar went up from the crowd and the man with the six stones was bought drinks by the winners.

The questions the old man asked were on all kinds of subjects. In what year did the Parce River dry up completely? Who defeated the Spanish general Annuire during the war of independence? When does the sun rise earlier, in May or September? Why is it dangerous to swim in the river on Good Friday? Sometimes there would be a series of questions on the same subject. For how long does a sow carry its young? How many young does a rabbit litter contain? Why does a rock snake sometimes not roll up at the approach of danger, but fold double instead? Sometimes the questions were about fruit. How many years does it take for a mango tree to bear its first fruit? When does the pith of a watermelon look yellow or even white, instead of red? Then he would move on to the Bible. How many children did Adam have? How many daughters did Adam have? How many sons did Noah have? How many livestock did Job have? Now and then he asked nonsense questions based on old wives' tales and superstitions. What did the donkey say to the tortoise under the tamarind tree? What was the king of Spain changed into when he failed to attend mass on Easter Sunday? His questions about folk medicine were particularly interesting. An infusion of the leaves of which plant can be taken against dysentery when you have torn off the leaves with a downward movement, and against vomiting if you have pulled them off with an upward motion? The fisherman's tobacco that grows on the rocks by the shore cures the clap, as we all know—after all, we're all men together—but what other illness does it cure? What fruit, mashed with olive oil, must be given for piles? Name three emetic plants.

When I got back to the farm it was already dark. At dinner I told them about what I had seen in the village. Sandoval laughed heartily. Her Majesty smiled benignly, but my blessed uncle thought the game was ridiculous—the villagers should concern themselves with more useful matters. He found the biblical questions about the number of daughters, sheep and goats particularly inane. Sandoval told us that one of his cows was about to calve. That morning, when he had taken his cattle from their cowshed and driven them to the meadow, he had noticed that the cow with calf was moving sluggishly and looked listless. Later in the day he saw that the cow had moved away from the others and kept sniffing the fence. He decided to take her back with him and put her in the little shed he called the "maternity ward." All day long, at regular intervals, he had gone to check on the cow, but she was still looking around in a daze. Calving could start any moment now. I said that I'd like to be present at the birth of a calf. Sandoval agreed immediately, but

I expected my uncle to be against the idea. Although he did frown a little, he decided it would be a good idea for me to witness one of God's miracles at close quarters.

There was another odd custom in Chimbarí, a very special way of settling disputes between neighbours. I did not see it myself, but was told about it in graphic detail by three youths whom I met on one of my walks near the little river at the edge of the village. All the women in the village, even the poorest, had two dresses that were worn on special occasions only: a green one that they put on to attend mass on Palm Sunday and kept on for the rest of the day, and a brilliant red one they wore when they argued with another woman. Whenever two women had a dispute, they would begin by giving each other a good tongue-lashing, exchanging the vilest insults for about half an hour. The woman who felt most offended would suddenly stop cursing and close all her doors and windows tight. This was a gross insult to the other party, as it meant the woman inside was no longer listening to what she was saying and could not be bothered to reply. In a rage, the woman left outside would put on her bright red dress, and usually a red headscarf too, and hurry to the riverbank. There she would reel of a litany of obscenities into the wind. She did this to attract the attention of the small boys who were usually playing by the river. Once she had their attention, she would let slip the name of her rival and tell them something awful about her. For example, that she played around with other men, that her mother had died of grief because her daughter had not looked after her, or that she had been caught in the market trying to slip a few bananas into her bag without paying. The boys would rush to the village to tell the woman in question what they had heard. Each boy knew it was his duty to do this—and there was reward attached to it too. When the defamed woman had listened to what the boys told her, she would start to complain loudly about the shame being heaped on her. She called on San Marco and his faithful lion to avenge her and gave each of the boys a cassava cake and sometimes a glass of syrup. The boys wolfed down their treats and hurried back to the river, anxious not to miss any of the fireworks to come. The second woman also put on her red dress and went to the river. When she arrived, she crossed the wooden bridge—this was nothing more than a plank with a railing, appropriately known as Me-First-Then-You—and took up her position on the far bank opposite her adversary. It was now her turn to do some insulting. She would claim that the whole village knew her opponent had lost her virginity long before her wedding day, that the priest had refused her communion on Easter Sunday two years previously, or that she had an illegitimate child who was being brought up by relatives in another village. These were mere preliminaries: the real slanging match now got under way. You can't imagine the things those boys told me! One woman said that her rival had an uncle behind bars in the Castillo, to which the rival replied that the woman had an aunt locked up in a lunatic asylum. Another woman said that her opponent's trip to Epifanía the previous year had not been to visit her son, but to have her rotting womb removed by a town doctor; in reply, the opponent accused her of having hard, unsightly lumps on her left breast. When it was her turn again, woman number one said that the woman on the opposite bank was frigid in bed, which is why her husband took the bus to Asunción every Saturday evening and did not come back until Sunday afternoon. To which number two retorted that, although she went around playing the *grande dame,* her husband was impotent, which is why her nerves were always on edge and she was so easily offended. Then they heard how the cousin of number two had been thrown out of the seminary in Crispo because of his filthy behaviour; a fine thing it would have been if that fellow had become a priest! Next, number one was informed that her niece was wandering around with VD at the age of thirteen. Meanwhile, half the population, most of them women and children, had turned out to watch the show. Everyone who came to the river had to take sides. Not surprisingly, relatives and friends of the women eagerly joined in the abuse. At dusk, groups of men came down to the river too, but they took no part in the dispute. They stayed in the background and passed the rum bottle from hand to hand. When darkness fell, the mudslinging began: balls of mud flew back and forth. The children made the projectiles at the water's edge and took them to the women, who hurled them across the river. Now the boys joined in too. In the darkness most of the mud balls missed their target, but every so often there was a direct hit and a new voice would launch into a new string of obscenities. The boys who told me the story were particularly keen on this mud warfare. One of them said that his own mother had once been a protagonist. "Did I throw some mud that night! I was walking around with a stiff arm for three days!" When it got really late, the performance came to an end. All the women had become hoarse by now and could produce only an in-comprehensible rattle. One camp would withdraw, followed a quarter of an hour later by their opponents. But sometimes when it got late, stones and slivers of glass were put in the mud balls, and if one of these nonstandard models hit the mark, the supporters of the injured person would rush across the bridge and there would be a general free-for-all. At this point the men would get involved and the party would end with a knife fight.

It was another day before Sandoval's cow gave birth. It was one-thirty in the morning when the little farmer came to wake me. "It's about to happen, but you don't have to come—you can stay in bed if you like." I quickly pulled on some trousers and followed him to the maternity ward. He had two oil lamps with him; one he hung on the wall, the other he placed on the ground next to the cow, which lay against the wall, clearly in labour. It would soon be calving, Sandoval said. Time passed, but the contractions still had no effect and the panting cow was becoming exhausted, so that Sandoval concluded that something was wrong. From that moment on he talked nonstop, explaining to me in the minutest detail what he was doing and why. He knelt down by the animal's hindquarters and, plunging two strong arms into the fleshy mass of its genitalia, pulled the lips apart. He could not see anything. He inserted a clenched fist into the orifice and slid his arm along the warm, slimy tunnel, deeper and deeper, until he could feel the head of the unborn calf. Slowly but powerfully he pushed against the wall of the tunnel with the back of his hand. At first he felt resistance, but then the wall of flesh gave way and his hand slid back over the calf's head. At that moment Sandoval grunted that he had a terrible pain in his back; his own stupid fault, he said, he shouldn't have started in a kneeling position, but should have lain full length on the floor before putting his arm in. But there was nothing to be done about it now, and with a great effort he shoved his arm even deeper into the cow. When his hand had found the folded front leg, which was protruding into the wall of the tunnel, he knew he had reached the right spot. Taking great care, so as not to break the fragile bones, he straightened the leg. As soon as the leg was in the correct position he felt the head of the calf slide forward a little way past his arm. He withdrew his arm until his hand was resting behind the head and waited. Then he felt the tunnel begin to contract again and as soon as the movement started, he carefully pulled the calf forward. After two more contractions Sandoval withdrew his arm completely from the cow. Nature would take its own course. It was not long before the animal's head appeared at the now gaping orifice and was thrust out. A little later the body of the calf slid onto the shed floor.

Relieved of her burden, the cow turned her head and licked Sandoval's bloody hand. The creature realised its mistake—perhaps it wasn't a mistake at all, but a token of gratitude?—and began licking the newborn calf clean. The calf dragged itself forward and the mother ran her tongue along its entire body. She then gave it a few prods, which made it slide even further forward; another shove and the calf was up on its feet. It was trembling all over. It slumped down, received another prod, got to its feet once more, but then collapsed again. Finally the calf stood up under its own power, wobbled, took a few uncertain steps backwards and fell against its mother's belly, its snout searching eagerly for the udder.

Sandoval watched with a smile and wiped his arm clean. Then he knelt down again and lifted a hind leg of the suckling creature with one hand and its tail with the other. Among the still-wet hairs he saw not two but only one orifice. He turned to me and said, happy and proud, "It's a bull! I'm damned if it isn't a bull!" I couldn't understand his enthusiasm. A new cow was more profitable, surely? Then he told me that twenty years earlier his wife had died giving birth to their only child. It was a daughter, who was now married and living in Crispo. And he confessed that he had always wanted a son. "Tonight my son was born!" he shouted, and burst out laughing.

Returning home on the train was less interesting and took longer than the outward journey. All was quiet once more in our town. A new *alcalde* had been appointed, a few troublemakers were in prison and the workers from the burnt-out factory were out of a job. Apart from that, everything was back to normal. Even the schools were open again. At home too, everything continued as before. Whenever I wanted a glass of water and opened the door of the fridge to get it, I saw a silver mug inside containing my uncle's spare dentures.

About six months earlier my uncle had come home one evening with his upper lip strangely caved in. He told us that for the first time in his life he had been to see a dentist, who was now in the process of extracting all the teeth from his upper jaw. He was to be fitted with a complete set of top dentures. I could hardly stop myself laughing at the strange hissing noise he made when he spoke. Sensibly, he had ordered two identical sets. "These things can break at any moment and then you're stuck. I can't keep interrupting my work to go to the dentist for new dentures. So I'm having two sets made at the same time." When he got his dentures, he put the spare set at the back of the fridge to protect them from dust and germs. This fridge was a wooden contraption lined with sheets of aluminium. Every day two large blocks of ice were placed on a grille and the space beneath was filled with bottles of water, meat and other food that needed to be kept cool. Although the false teeth were not visible when you opened the door, you could see the mug. I often slammed the fridge shut without drinking a thing.

Two months after our stay on Sandoval's farm my uncle's wife died. He came home earlier than usual, and I realised at once that something was wrong, because he did not take off his hat until he got to the middle of the room and then wiped his neck and brow with a handkerchief and placed the hat on a chair. His unvarying nightly routine was to take his hat off as he came through the front door, hang it on the top peg of the coat rack just inside, and only then wipe his neck and brow. My uncle quickly realised he had departed from his usual routine, so he went back to the chair, picked up the hat and hung it on the peg. Then he wiped his forehead and neck a second time.

He sat down on the big sofa and motioned me to sit next to him. He put his arm round my shoulders and asked if I had heard about the train crash that afternoon near Crispo. No, I knew nothing about it. Then he said softly, "A terrible disaster. Twenty-nine people were killed. Your aunt was one of the victims." At first I didn't understand what he meant. Had a sister of my father or mother come to the mainland and been killed in the train crash? He saw my confusion and said even more softly, "My wife, my dear wife has departed this life."

When I heard this, I cried and expected him to do the same. But he hugged me and said in an almost accusing tone, "It is God's will. We must be strong at a time like this. He knows what He's doing, even when we can't fathom His mystery." At that moment I conceived a great dislike of the man who was hugging me. How could anyone talk so coolly when his own wife had died a terrible death a few hours before?

After the death of his wife, while I was waiting for a ship back to my island, I had to sleep in my uncle's room, although I could not see why this was necessary. My narrow bed was placed in a corner of the huge room. It was a cheerless place with spotless linoleum on the floor, containing my uncle's enormous bed with a tall chair at its foot, a washbasin with strange curled legs and a solid mahogany wardrobe with a brass keyhole plate. On the white walls hung two paintings, one a portrait of some nineteenth-century preacher who had been killed and probably eaten by an Indian tribe — he served as a model to my uncle — and the other a depiction of the Last Supper, or as my uncle called it, "Our Lord's Holy Supper." Many homes have a Last Supper hanging in the dining room, but here it was in the bedroom, right at the foot of my bed, so that I was forced to gaze at it every evening. On the print I could identify only Jesus and Judas — Iscariot, as my uncle called him — but he could name all thirteen figures from right to left. I've never understood how my uncle could be so sure who was who. I preferred the preacher in the other picture, with his flabby face, shifty stare and silly hat.

When my uncle came to bed, he always opened the door of the

bedroom carefully, shuffled in and put the light on. I would wake with a start and he would say in surprise, "What, aren't you asleep yet? Boys need lots of sleep if they're to grow up healthy." Then he would take his neatly folded pyjamas from the foot of the bed, draping first the trousers and then the jacket over his left arm, and shuffle out of the room again. It was ten minutes or so before he reappeared, now in his pyjamas, with the jacket buttoned right up to his Adam's apple. "What, are you still not asleep, my boy?" He smoothed out the clothes he had just taken off and hung them over the chair by his bed. Next, he ran his fingertips over his veined temples and pressed his eyelids with his forefingers. Then he climbed into bed and lay flat on his back in the very middle. Not long after I heard his heavy breathing, punctuated by horrid rasping sounds. As a child I firmly believed that all good Christians slept straight as a die in the middle of the bed and that all of them snored.

Six weeks later I was on a ship taking me home. I felt rather seasick during the twelve-hour journey, though this had never happened on my previous crossings. Dizzy and slightly nauseous, I sat on the stiff canvas seat of a deck chair. Then I heard the sound of wings. A large, grubby-white bird fluttered along and perched on the deck rail. Its belly and feet were covered in oil. It had a long beak with a pocket attached and looked as old as the world. Only its eyes glittered as it gazed at me with curiosity. As I in turn studied the bird closely, it suddenly dawned on me what I had learned from the thin prisoner in the Castillo: he had shown me without words how to look at birds and plants differently, to see details that most people miss. And despite the unpleasant taste of vomit in my mouth I was overcome by a faint sense of elation and gratitude. I drew up my knees and arched my back against the canvas, then stuck my thumb in my mouth and sucked it like a little child until I fell asleep.

SEVEN

On this island, when a white man outlives his white wife there is often a black woman waiting for him. When he has become a widower, lonely and less of a man, there is always the black woman who receives him with open arms and cares for him lovingly during his declining years.

As I sit on my terrace, half-drunk and brooding on my solitude, the night is my black woman. In the embrace of her strong cinnamon arms I feel at once dominant and protected. Her ancient face has a rough beauty as inextinguishable as the wild north coast, with its rocky monuments carved out by sea and wind. Her eyes, wise but tired from her long vigil, gaze endlessly at a mysterious image, a compound of emptiness, mystery and long distances, that I will never fathom. How often, night after night, I have basked in her silken black embrace. The scent of her black woman's body merges dream and reality, blurs the outlines of earthly things into insignificant shadows, and blots out the false world and its threats. I press my back against her huge breasts and when the warmth of her flesh transmits itself to my skin I can erase all scarring memories at a stroke. Then I caress her knees and full of gratitude call her the guardian of my drunken nights. And I ask her, although I know she will never reply: have I ever been happy?

The ethereal moon has slid away among the clouds. I take another swig of whisky and listen to the rustling of the creatures that live in the blackness of the night. The great death's head moth on the side of the flowerpot must have shifted imperceptibly, because it is now in a different position. It has sat there for hours, neither moving nor showing any interest in my presence. Even when I have occasionally got up, to replenish my supply of liquor or relieve myself of the beer I have imbibed, it has not moved but has sat glued to the concrete pot, its wings fully extended, its head, with a tiny glistening jewel set in it, pointing downwards. In popular superstition it is a harbinger of death and, like death, its scientific name, *Erebus odora,* is both poetic and ominous. It's strange that people should associate the insect with death, whereas the butterfly is the symbol of immortality. It's called the black death's head moth, but now the light is falling on it and you can see that it is not black but dark brown. I did not see it move, but its head is now pointing upwards. Is it preparing to take off? Perhaps that would be best. I do find it slightly unnerving having to sit for several hours less than two yards away from a death's head.

My bitch Fonda, who has also kept me company for hours, lying loyally at my feet, stretches and raises her head for a few minutes, her eyes focused on a single point in the sky. Then she rotates several times on the spot, as always when she is about to sleep; she does not lie down, however, but begins to rub her body against my knees. I can't decide whether she is being playful or has been alarmed by something. I stroke her and notice that the skin on her head and neck is taut. At that moment something brushes past, making me start momentarily. At first I assume it is the death's head flying off, but the moth is still sitting on the flowerpot as serene and motionless as ever. The thing passes again and now I see that it is a second death's head moth. That is very odd, since one never sees two of these insects together. They always deliver their notifications of death alone. The moth on the flowerpot releases its hold and tumbles downwards, but just before hitting the ground it flutters upwards and joins its companion. The two of them fly back and forth. I follow them intently and suddenly discover that there are four moths hovering around. Am I so drunk that I'm seeing double? I finish my whisky and now see six—no, eight—moths in the air. The swarm keeps growing and I can no longer count them, but there must be at least twenty death's heads in flight. I'm not particularly superstitious, but this spectacle is taking things a little too far.

If you suspect a disaster or a miracle is imminent, you must prepare. This situation calls for a stiff drink. I go indoors and for the first time the dog comes with me, pressing her body against my legs and almost making me stumble, since I'm seldom very steady on my feet by this hour. I decide to take a brand-new bottle of whisky outside. This goes against all my drinking principles. I have always stuck to the system of getting up and going inside to pour a new drink, which is a good way of regulating my intake. But this is a special night and the usual rules don't apply. As tender as a mother cradling her infant, I carry the whisky bottle out to the terrace. I forget the beer; this is no time for soft drinks. Sometimes you have to be drunk to understand what's going on around you. There are things in life, and beyond life, that you can make contact with only when you've lost all sense of heaven and earth.

Back on the terrace, I cannot believe my eyes. A gently undulating sea of hundreds of death's head moths is washing incessantly and almost silently over the garden. Only when the swarm flies into the wind is there a faint rushing sound like running water. I sit down, feeling rather uneasy. Do moths attack people? What if those stupid insects take it into their heads to descend on me all at once? I put my hand on Fonda's neck; her body is as hard as stone. She is sitting up, straight-backed and motionless, apart from jerking her head slightly to the left and right as the moths fly past, like someone following a table tennis match. I rub her neck and back more vigorously, but it's like stroking a marble statue. Perhaps it would be best to switch off the light at the front of my house; the swarm might fly off then. Moths are obviously telepathic, for when they surge past me, they do not turn when they reach the end of the fence — as they had done hundreds of times before — but continue straight on. They do not return. The garden is now empty and deathly quiet. The dog lies down at my feet and closes its eyes. I take a stiff drink and wonder who will have the task of placing the ten-cent piece for Charon under the tongues of the corpses of the hundreds, perhaps thousands, of islanders who will die tonight?

I must make the best possible use of the respite granted me by the moths' departure. I decide to go inside for a shower. It is the first time in my life that I've showered at two in the morning. The water is ice cold and I feel like drying off quickly and forgoing my intended ablutions. But with a drunk's stubbornness I persevere. I turn the tap on full so that the water lashes down on my head. After a few minutes it no longer feels as cold. I shampoo my hair thoroughly, twice, as recommended on the bottle: once to remove the dirt, then a good rinse, and the second time to make the hair shine and the scalp tingle with freshness. Then I soap my whole body, paying special attention to the ears, the tender part under the foreskin, and the toes. Astonishingly, I start to enjoy it: after rinsing myself down, I let the water gush over my head for several more minutes. I dry myself thoroughly and sprinkle my armpits and groin with talc. As I am combing my hair in front of the mirror, I notice that I badly need a shave. That is quickly done. I remove the stubble carefully, as I have an innate respect for razors. With a small pair of scissors I also clip the few hairs protruding from my nose and ears. Next, sitting on the lid of the toilet, I cut both fingernails and toenails. Finally I put on clean clothes: all white, underwear as well as trousers and shirt. Right then. Ready for the wedding and for the coffin, as I've sometimes heard it said of someone dressed immaculately.

I go back outside feeling both physically and mentally rejuvenated. The effect of the alcohol seems to have been largely washed away by the shower, so that I can begin again with new zest. Strange how physical cleansing can create the illusion that your soul is also being purified. I feel like the leading man in a play who has taken off his makeup after the show and is himself once again — and I succumb to an overpowering urge to understand myself completely. I sit down in my old place on the terrace and nestle in the lap of my black woman, who has waited passively for my return. She is the all-comprehending Holy Caribbean Mother, the slut who has eagerly received many a snow-white penis in her black belly. My hands clasp her knees, my forearms rest on her thighs and my back lies on the great water bed of her softly yielding breasts.

Without moving the rest of my body, I grope cautiously for the whisky bottle with my left hand. Gripping the neck of the bottle with three fingers, I unscrew the cap with my thumb and forefinger. I put the bottle to my lips and take two swigs in succession, a serious departure from the standard method for polishing off whisky. I feel a new warmth in my chest and press my body more firmly against my woman. She reciprocates by putting her black arms around me and squeezing her thighs together, making me feel almost claustrophobic. My lower back is clamped against the warm slit between her legs and I can feel the throb and pull of her ancient vulva. Little spasms of exaltation travel through my body as in a diffuse orgasm.

But whenever a man and a woman are together, even in a make-believe nocturnal paradise, they hear the writhing and hissing of accursed, shambling creatures. Every spark of the human spirit has its antidote, every sensory delight a grain of venom. Again and again, whenever a feeling of contentment starts to well up in me, it is overwhelmed by a snapping sound that crudely tarnishes everything.

I start to feel that certain organs in my body have speeded up their functions. My blood is pounding wildly through my brain and is being sucked from my head in torrents; my temples are pressing inwards. I become dizzy and hear a deep male voice intoning a rapid singsong prayer, occasionally interspersed with children's voices in short, uneven bursts. A small bell tinkles and after a brief silence a monotonous hymn rises from the throats of hundreds of schoolboys in the playground. I see myself hurrying to an empty classroom and taking the teacher's telescope from the cupboard. I return to my hiding place behind the flower tubs in the corridor and, unseen, follow the progress of the ceremony down below. I put the telescope to my eye, but I do not see my classmates taking communion; the playground is empty. I realise I am using the instrument the wrong way round and have pushed everything and everyone far away from me. I am utterly alone.

I feel I'm starting to fall apart and at the same time have the sensation of myself being at the other end of the telescope, observing myself through the narrower aperture and gazing into my own enormous eyes. Through the transparent cornea of those eyes I can see how the beams of light are refracted and then projected onto the retina as images of the outside world. But I myself *am* the outside world, because I am at both ends of the telescope. I can see the reflections of that other world that have been retained by the retina, but the pigment cells have recorded only banal images, nicely rounded representations that are of no use at times like this. I want to look more deeply inside myself, past the myriad fibres of the optic nerve into that soft, never-resting mass that regulates our bodily functions and mental processes, where the protozoic and the divine soul eternally cohabit and generate all my actions. I want to decipher the architecture of the cells that so arrogantly determine the pattern of my life, to decode the circuit of impulses that manipulate me like a puppet, to enter the territory of my body's creator and ask him timidly for some explanations.

As usual, every attempt to understand myself fails, every yearning for God is punished. I hear the telescope smash to pieces on the
tiled floor of the corridor, disrupting the celebration of mass in the
playground. I am dragged roughly back to my terrace and my knees
start to go weak. The dizziness worsens. I need a stiff drink but don't
have the guts to reach for the bottle.

On the news this afternoon it said you can see a star exploding
in the night sky with the naked eye—an explosion that took place
170,000 years ago. I realise how ridiculous it was of me just now
when I presumed to crave a few minutes' attention from the Ruler
of the Universe. I force myself to grab the bottle and put it to my lips.
The merciful liquid brings the constantly metamorphosing hills in
front of me back into focus. I hear again the girlish cries of the small
birds of prey that sail along on the wind like children at play. Why
lick wounds that never heal, mourn what's over and done with or
boast of sins only cowardice stopped you committing?

The nausea and weakness disappear. I feel almost cheerful and
look with renewed interest at the splash of blood on the garden
path. The oblong stain, which looks like a map of Italy, has dried
up completely; it has gone dark brown and occasionally gives off a
sickly smell. Yesterday afternoon I slipped up when changing guard
dogs, and the two males that hate each other most came face to face.
Not for long. With terrifying growls and dingo-like battle cries they
flew at each other with a ferocity I had not expected of my faithful domestic companions. I managed to end the furious duel quite
quickly by drenching them both with the garden hose. One of the
dogs had received a nasty bite in its neck which was bleeding pro-

fusely. I rubbed lots of red ointment from the magic tube onto the wound and the bleeding stopped. Of course, I should have hosed the pool of blood off the path at once, but I didn't bother. When the cruel tormenting spirit passes through the land on its tenth circuit and sees this bloodstain, it may pass over my house in silence and proceed to my neighbour's, where it will slay the eldest son.

EIGHT

There has never been a night so perfect for undergoing a cleansing baptism. Or for dying. Surely it must have been here on my terrace, sitting on the same paving slab, that Baudelaire, thoroughly depraved and hell-bent on destroying his health, stinking drunk but blessed with an inner clarity, was moved to create that unsurpassed line:

> With neither smile nor tear do I disturb
> the calm at which I gaze . . .

When in fifteen minutes' time a last jolt brings to an end all life on earth, there will be nothing left, no evil or beauty, and eternal calm will descend. I spend the remaining minutes staring straight ahead in melancholy exhaustion.

And I see the German with the red beard who called on me a few months back. He trained as a paediatrician, but is now a famous anthropologist who visits the remotest corners of South America on strange assignments from scientific institutions in Europe. He tells me he once saw a group of boys playing football with an old tin can. On the next expedition he took with him twelve brightly coloured rubber balls which he distributed to children. He gave away the last ball in a native village close to the source of the Pauchua River, to a group of small boys wandering around naked. Each of them had a protruding navel longer than the little penis dangling from his abdomen. The ball passed from hand to hand. The boys sniffed it and held it to their ears. They shook it, stroked it, tapped it and squeezed it. The last boy took a quick lick and with a bashful laugh returned it to the red-haired *Übermensch*. The boys did not know what a ball was. They had never heard of football.

And I see other children. Little girls trudging the streets with jute sacks on their backs, rummaging through dustbins for discarded bottles they can hand in at the lemonade factory for a few cents each. Boys of eight with grey-rimmed eyes who chew certain leathery leaves that they know dull the hunger and make them pleasantly light-headed. A little boy sitting by the roadside stubbornly trying to blow up into a balloon a condom he has found in an open sewer. Children with permanently tear-stained faces and children who never cry, children with huge suspicious eyes, others with empty, watery ones. Children with scabby sores on their heads, hands and feet; with eternally snotty noses; with open wounds and oozing boils and hair that has never been combed. Children who scratch incessantly, who go round with dried shit on their buttocks and thighs, constantly pursued by flies. A boy sitting hunched on a step in the sweltering afternoon sun, hugging his chest because he has the shivers.

And I look up to the summit of the Andes, to where, just below the dwelling of the real god, the god of South America dwells in his palace of blue ice on 23,390-foot Aconcagua, from where he can survey the whole continent. Each morning, after he has made the sun rise, he commands his angels to unbolt the heavenly gates of the palace and lower the ivory drawbridge so that he can stride out along the cloudy walls of his palace and glance down dutifully at the silver shimmer of sunlight on the mountain ridges and at the suffering below. But after a few hundred years these morning walks start to disturb him and his gentleman-in-waiting notices that each day he returns from his stroll more depressed. The faithful servant becomes even more concerned when a member of the angelic host guarding the ramparts tells him he has heard the god muttering, "Sadness and guilt pierce my heart," and that another sentry heard him whisper, "All misery ceases when one no longer knows that misery exists." One evil day, the god looks down on his domain and sees the profound sorrow that fills the valley below, the deceit that clings to the trees and the impotent rage that lies buried in human hearts. He hears the lamentation that drifts up the slopes from the poor, of whom there will never be a shortage in the land, from the eternal prisoners and those who have disappeared without trace. On that day, all the benevolent spirits that inhabit the palace shudder at their master's lament on the ramparts: "If this wall were not a cloud of floating ice crystals I would throw myself on my back and look skywards for ever. Or I would turn on my stomach and bury my face in the grass." The gentleman-in-waiting, whose task it is to please the Lord of Heaven in everything, hastily summons the other four archangels—the chief footman, the vizier, the wine steward and the stable master—to a meeting. This emergency meeting of the palace council is a long and busy one. The following morning, when the golden gate is opened and the god ventures wearily outside to be irritated by the glittering interplay of sun and snow and by the suffering down below, his youngest page approaches diffidently yet respectfully down an azure corridor and, genuflecting, offers him a crimson-lacquered golden casket. The god, taken by surprise, opens the casket: nested on a snow-white satin cushion embroidered with silver doves is a pair of spectacles, its lenses set in diamond frames and thinly coated with lead on both sides. He carefully puts on the glasses and finds it hard to suppress a smile. He puts out his hand and says to the page, "Lead me to the ramparts." When he arrives at the walls, he looks down and allows a smile to appear on his lips. "They're rather heavy on the nose," he tells the page in a kindly voice, "but I shall never take them off again." He gropes for the boy's head, bends down and bestows a grateful kiss on the cheek of the perplexed cherub.

And I see four armoured trucks containing a hundred and fifty soldiers smash through Fernando's wooden gate and drive into his yard. They stop outside the little house. Fernando and his wife wake with a start. Their daughter comes charging into their room and flings herself into her mother's arms. Fernando pulls the blinds halfway down: "*Dios mío*, the soldiers are here." Rattling off some quick prayers to the patron saint of farmers, mother and daughter get dressed. Fernando doesn't need to: he always sleeps in the same worn khaki trousers he wears during the day, their frayed legs not quite reaching his ankles. He doesn't put a shirt on, but dons his broad-brimmed hat as protection against the evening dew. "Whatever happens, you two stay inside. Understood?" His authoritative tone makes the fear in the women's eyes fade a little, for they rec-

ognise in his words the same self-confidence they have always admired in this taciturn, hardworking husband and father. "God go
with you," whispers his wife, and his daughter is about to say something too when they hear the pounding of rifle butts against the
front door. Fernando quickly closes the bedroom door behind him.
In the kitchen he stops for a moment and looks through the gloom
at the pots and pans hanging on the wall, the massive sink under the
pump and the barrel of drinking water in the corner. "My God," he
groans, "I'm taking leave of the things in my house." He hurries out.
He is caught in the light of scores of torches and shields his eyes with
his hands. He is a pathetic spectacle, with his half-length trousers,
his broad-brimmed hat, his skinny rib cage and his hairy armpits glistening with beads of anxious sweat. "He's still sweating!" he hears
someone shout. "He's sweating from every pore," screams someone
else. "Perhaps he was screwing that old whore of his." "His old prick
hasn't been up to that for ages!" "Then he must have been licking
her, the dirty swine." "But not his wife's twat, the filthy slob was at
his daughter's virgin slit!" Fernando is scarcely able to think: these
aren't people, they're a bunch of animals. He considers praying, not
to his patron saint, but directly to God. He has often criticised the
exaggerated piety of his wife, who is constantly lighting candles and
making novenas to obtain some favour. God and his saints don't concern themselves with everyday matters, he would say; they mustn't
be pestered with trifling problems. They are there for the times in
your life when you really need help, such as marriage or death. And
for disasters such as fire, earthquake or floods. But Fernando cannot pray now, as he needs to devote all his attention to what is hap-

pening around him. There are moments when God abandons one of his own, he says without moving his lips. The lord and master of heaven and earth has deserted him, and in his place a short, fat figure approaches. Made omnipotent by the hundred and fifty soldiers around him, this man is now lord and master over the lives of Fernando and his wife and daughter. He comes mincing towards Fernando, who, lit by the torches, stands on the steps of his house like an actor in the spotlight. "I am Captain Román. Good evening, Fernando Pirela." "Good evening, *mi capitán.*" Fernando is amazed that his voice does not shake. It quickly dawns on him that the captain addressed him by name and that the soldiers know he has a wife and daughter; so they haven't come bursting in here on an off chance. "Fernando, it isn't polite to hold your hands over your eyes when you're talking to someone." Fernando drops his hands. The beams of several torches are now being directed at his face and he cannot keep his eyes open. "Nor is it right, Fernando, to keep your eyes shut when you're talking to someone." Fernando blinks and half-opens his eyes. He cannot see Román, the soldiers or the night at all; just the yellow globes of the torches dancing before his eyes. "Fernando. Do I have to look up to you?" He squats down. This is a relief, as he is not sure whether his legs will carry him for much longer. "Christ! Look at the balls on that one!" shouts one of the soldiers. "It's a wonder he can still walk with those swollen bollocks!" Another soldier joins in: "I bet his wife's black and blue from all that humping between her thighs!" With a motion of his hand Captain Román silences his men. "No, Fernando, you mustn't squat when I'm talking to you. Don't you think it's more polite to the military authorities to kneel?" The peasant fights back a momentary impulse to leap on Román and tear him apart with his bare hands and teeth. The soldiers will gun him down and it will all be over. But what will happen to his wife and daughter then? He sinks to his knees.

"Good. You're an obedient man. So I expect you're a good citizen too, aren't you?"

"Certainly, captain."

"A citizen who obeys all the laws of his country?"

"Of course, captain."

"Ha, so we're dealing with a model citizen. Tell me, have you got any cows?"

"Sí, capitán."

"And goats?"

"Sí, capitán."

"What do you do with those cows and goats?"

"I sell the milk, captain."

"Who to?"

"To the co-operative depot in Pueblo Nuevo."

"Who else?"

"No one else, captain. I have to deliver all milk to the depot."

"Don't you sell milk to your neighbours?"

"Neighbours? I haven't got any near neighbours, captain. The nearest place, Sanchez's . . ."

"I mean your neighbours in the jungle!"

"In the jungle? I don't understand you, captain."

"No. of course you don't understand me. But what about meat? Don't you sell meat? Don't you ever slaughter one of your cows?"

"Oh no, captain. I live on my cow's milk. Later, when my young bull is fully grown and my cows start calving, I may be able to slaughter a cow now and then and sell the meat. I hope to live to see the day."

"I hope so too. No, I'm sure of it. Before you die you'll see your cows slaughtered. You mark my prophetic words!"

The interrogation continues for quite a while. Suddenly Captain Román has had enough and orders Fernando to go to his cow pen: "That's where you belong, among the dumb animals!" A dozen soldiers climb onto the wall of the open pen and at Román's command the automatic weapons start rattling. Then Fernando's wife is raped five times and his daughter ten times. The two women are tied to their beds and the house is set alight. The farmer's little house burns to the ground and the soldiers leave. A slender moon appears among the clouds and casts a faint light on the dismal scene. Only the front wall of the burnt-out farmhouse is still standing; occasionally there is a crackling sound from the smouldering ruins. In the pen the body of the peasant lies among his dead cows, some of which are still bleeding. The whole scene has the desolate air of the paintings of Sergio Etchechourry, the visionary artist who over a century ago immortalised the War of Independence, and particularly the struggle in the countryside, in scenes of ghastly devastation and death. The farmers in the wide plain of Tierra Baja learned their lesson. None of them would ever again take it into their head to supply meat, milk or eggs to the guerrilla camp in the jungle.

And I see a nineteen-year-old youth dressed in dark blue jeans, white T-shirt and trainers who, from the third-floor balcony of a house in the Calle Principal throws a grenade at a military vehicle which drives down the street every day at 12:03 pm carrying twenty men of the National Guard to the Los Reyes barracks. Either from youthful insouciance or from anxiety because he is carrying out his first terrorist attack, the man lobs the projectile with far too much force. The grenade sails right over the vehicle and explodes in the gateway of the school on the other side of the street, just at the moment when the children come rushing out. Seven boys and girls are killed instantly, thirteen are injured. The soldiers immediately cordon off the street and search the houses; the weeping culprit is caught. He keeps screaming that the grenade was meant for the military vehicle. Under torture at the barracks he reveals which group he belongs to, who sent him on the mission, and how he got hold of the grenade. The radio stations broadcast classical music for three days, occasionally interrupted by a new report of the confessions of the grenade thrower or an interview with the next of kin of the little victims. The funeral takes place on Sunday afternoon, and as the sad cortège crosses the Plaza del Sol, the two fountains spout water dyed red to symbolise the spilling of innocent blood. The following morning the grenade thrower's head is displayed on the pinnacle of one of the fountains. The eyeless head hangs there until the skin has turned black. One morning it has gone and the Plaza del Sol is officially renamed the Plaza de los Niños.

And I see a Caribbean island with big hotels and white beaches newly replenished with shining sand. In a little house an old woman prays to her favourite saint for the safety of her son. He has been in Europe for a year; he likes it fine and is earning good money. It's

true he hasn't sent any home, but she is happy with his cheerful letters, which she reads ten times over. But Europe is a very big island
where rich people live. They have gold mines and apartheid and
nuclear rockets they have borrowed from America and will fire at
each other when they declare war. She has read all that with her own
eyes in the morning paper. The gold mines have long, dark tunnels
that reach the centre of the earth. But the Europeans don't go down
themselves, they send in black West Indians and Turks to extract
the gold. From time to time, one of the tunnels caves in and buries
many workers. That is why she is praying for her son. Her prayer is
not heard. His body is fished out of a canal by the police and press reports say he was murdered by drug dealers. The story appears under
splash headlines in her morning paper. The old woman never knew
that the Pope had declared many years earlier that Santa Filomena
was not a true saint.

And I see my garden gate swing open and Eugenio, once a
schoolteacher and now the village idiot, enters. As he comes into
the light I can see that he is not wearing his customary hat or the
boots in which he keeps newspaper cuttings. His trousers are rolled
up to just below the knee and I notice that he has six toes on his
left foot. That is to say, above his little toe there is an appendage
that looks very like a miniature toe. When he has come very close,
he startles me by suddenly tumbling forward and standing on his
head. With his head and hands on the ground and his legs flailing
to keep his balance, he starts bellowing in the annoying, singsong
way of children reciting a prayer or a poem: "A person could go old
and grey with all that waiting! Who was it promised a land of milk

and honey? That the blind would see? The deaf hear? A thousand-year land of plenty? Meanwhile, take pity on the rich—millionaires can be unhappy too—comfort the strong—tough guys also sometimes lose—forget the Third World—send consolation to the capitalists—and please don't forget the white folks because of all those blacks. Ignore the sick, the prisoners, the lonely—award a title to a successful prostitute—increase the robber's haul—give the terrorists a hand—democrats can stand on their own feet, so let's do something for a fascist government. The conservationists, the disabled, the elderly and the homosexuals get quite enough attention as it is, so let's give healthy people more vitality—turn all the water into wine again, drunks are the salt of the earth! All those kids who masturbate on the sly, give them exciting fantasies—and while we're talking about children, let all the pompous schoolmasters suffocate in their sleep—or if that's not possible, then let the Holy Ghost reveal the exam questions in advance. Let a notary win the jackpot in the lottery—bless all royal houses—give every prince a beautiful princess—give a bonus to every rapist—encourage the sadomasochists and the Christian Socialists too—let landslides and volcanic eruptions happen only in poor, densely populated regions—no more trains full of suntanned tourists must be derailed. Anoint those in authority—be particularly munificent to dictators, slave owners and the CIA—give bigger profits to drug dealers and more oil to the Arabs—give us a pope who is thirty, as well as thirty pieces of silver for everyone—strengthen the arm of the executioner—give the pyromaniac a steady hand—and don't forget all the majorities. Organise a gigantic festival where smugglers and alcoholics, usurers and politicians, chain-smokers and tax dodgers, bank managers and atheists, environmental polluters and pornographers, plane hijackers and book reviewers, pickpockets and child molesters can win cups and gold medals!"

And I see my garden gate swing open a second time, and now it is the black trade union leader coming towards me. He used to be pugnacious and full of fire, but now he has grown older and more circumspect. He invites me to accompany him. We go to the city and enter a large jeweller's shop. There is thick wall-to-wall carpeting that muffles our footsteps; all you can hear is the hubbub of customers and sales assistants. Silver, gold and diamonds gleam at us from all sides. We see showcases piled high with Swiss watches and others with huge, glistening diamond earrings, the kind that hang from the ears of Imelda Marcos, and glittering bracelets that might jingle on the skinny arms of Michèle Duvalier. In the wall cases we see exquisite porcelain figurines depicting tender scenes of little lambs and flowers, frail wenches and tubercular young men. Amid this serene beauty, the trade union leader gives me a dig in the ribs and winks. In his hoarse voice he shouts, "Ladies and gentlemen, your attention please." Then he lets out a ferocious and deafening fart that makes the glass of the showcases shake and the little carillon on the shop front tinkle out of tune. The powdered and perfumed tourists, many fitted with pacemakers, rush outside and scream hysterically for taxis to take them to the airport, to the safety of New York and the decorum of Boston.

And I see a boy and his uncle going for a walk in the woods. "Nothing better than a day in God's fresh air to give you a second wind and put fresh heart into you," says the uncle. The woods are dense and silent.

"Won't we get lost?" asks the boy.

"God is our compass," is the answer. The boy is tired because he has to carry a basket full of oranges, large, hard biscuits and religious magazines. "Can't we rest a bit?"

"That's a good idea. Come on, let's sit down by that big tree trunk."

The uncle takes the basket and puts his arm round the boy's shoulders, but with a quick movement the boy ducks underneath the arm and sits down on a boulder some way away. It is no longer silent in the woods. The boy hears the grating sound of wheelbarrows being pushed up and down, and further on there is the sound of a mill crushing stones. The trunks of the giant trees begin to expand sideways; they grow wider and wider until they touch each other and seal off a whole section of the woods from the rest of the world. The sound of the squeaking wheels, the mill and the pickaxes striking the ground grows louder. Next to him on the boulder sits a man staring patiently straight ahead, always at the same spot. He is as thin as a rake. The boy has never seen such a skinny adult before, but what fascinates him most are the large grey eyes, as expressionless as those of a blind man. The boy has the strange, mystifying sensation that the man is not in fact staring straight ahead, but that his gaze is focused backwards and inwards. "Hello, sir." "Hello, boy." The voice is flat and toneless, and as the man utters the two words he makes a gesture with his bony left hand as if ordering the din around him to stop. The boy thinks that he is perhaps the only person in the whole world who can hear the man, and he wants to get up and bring him an orange from his uncle's basket. But he decides not to because he will be hurt if the man doesn't accept the fruit. The man lights a cigarette, inhaling deeply and without pleasure. He wears prison clothes, the blue-and-white-striped overall open from neck to navel exposing his rib cage. The two rows of thin ribs are very pronounced and the indentations between them are dark in colour; there is a deep groove from his throat to just above his navel. "Your body is like Christ's on the cross," says the boy, but immediately regrets saying it. The man's face is inscrutable. Is he annoyed or amused? I'd better say something else quickly, thinks the boy—but what am I supposed to talk about to someone who says nothing himself and perhaps can't even hear what I'm saying? For all I know, he may be deaf. Deaf and blind, and so full of fear and uncertainty and terribly lonely. "I sometimes feel unhappy too," he could have said to the man to comfort him, but what he actually says is, "There's my perfect uncle. Do you see him over there by that big tree trunk? According to him, everything is sinful or leads to sin." The boy is ashamed of having said that; the man probably found his words just as funny as his previous remark about his Christ-like body. "I want to change as quickly as possible and become a man with broad shoulders and strong arms and legs, and I shall grow a moustache." The man has a cigarette end in his mouth and his thin lips move only when he blows out the smoke. Then the boy suddenly imagines that he hears words, spoken with the gasping voice of someone with a lung disease. The boy listens attentively, but cannot quite grasp the meaning of the words. "Happy expectations of the future and fond memories of the past are both treacherous things. We are all criminals: half of us are already in prison uniform, while the acolytes are still in white cassocks. One man does penance for his sins, another still carries his misdeeds covertly around with him. We don't know what's in store for us and later we will never know what happened to us. I too was once ten years old." The man takes the cigarette end, no more than half an inch long, out of his mouth, pulls a new cigarette out of his breast pocket and lights it from the previous one. The boy observes him from the side. The man looks weak and emaciated, but at the same time wiry and tough; he has something about him of a wild animal that has just mauled and eaten a weaker creature. The boy feels that he must say something: "I wish *you* were my uncle." He is shocked by his own words, not because of what he said, but because he addressed the man so familiarly—this man his uncle called a thug whose soul was doomed to burn in hellfire for all eternity.

Wait . . . the old indju tree in my garden sighs and the cool night wind caresses its bony arms for the last time, lisping words of consolation. When in nine minutes' time I am dead, when my heart no longer beats in my cold body and my soul is already in the hereafter, the watch on my wrist will go on ticking for hours.

NINE

The days and years have all been lived and have crumbled to dust. I am cocooned by the final night, uncertain of what heavenly bliss and hellish pains lie beyond the horizon. At the mercy of an alien will, yet at the same time strengthened by an unsuspected reserve of courage that derives from my drinking, I await unrepentantly for whatever else the night may bring—and still there are surges of a will to live. I look up at the ebony ramparts of heaven, but on the far side of the hemisphere the knives are already out. Fragile angels with flashing swords they can barely lift are quite calmly searing away what is engraved in the book of nature. By the light of billions of yellow candles I hear the cosmic silence shattered by the death rattle of all earthly dreams and the howl of frightened dogs.

I pick up the whisky bottle, which is still half full, and unscrew the cap. I hold the bottle upside down over the flowerpot and with a pang of guilt see the noble liquid greedily absorbed by the bone-dry earth. Just before the bottle is completely empty, I quickly turn it upright and place it between my feet on the terrace. I strike a match and drop it carefully into the bottle. The last drops of alcohol ignite immediately and a small blue flame spurts up through the neck of the bottle with a soft hum. Just when almost everything has burnt up and the fire is dying down, I close off the mouth of the bottle with the palm of my hand. The flame goes out at once and the bottle fills with smoke. I slowly raise my arm and the bottle follows, stuck to my palm. This drunkard's party piece is called "conjuring the genie out of the bottle." I detach the bottle from my hand, neatly replace its cap and with a powerful swing hurl it across the garden, over the road and into the undergrowth on the other side. Keep Your Island Clean! The slogan of the sanitation department doesn't apply tonight.

I extend my right arm so that the light from the lamp falls on it: there is a small pink circle on the inside of my hand. I'm a marked man. Then I extend my left hand, so that the light catches my wristwatch.

It is 2:46 am—and at that moment the water level changes in all the wells and springs on the Caribbean islands and the South American mainland. All domestic pets grow restless; in the towns the rats flee noiselessly from the sewer; and in the snow-covered southern regions of the continent animals with faded coats awaken prematurely from hibernation. The firmament is now strewn with stars; the earth is being sympathetically observed by millions of fiery eyes.

The sound of a distant waterfall, at first a murmur, becomes louder and more ominous, like the grumbling of a god who has decided to exterminate everything that lives. The fear and terror of the falling water is conveyed like feverish painting on the wind. The message is picked up and understood by a cricket at the top of the indju tree in my garden and it immediately passes on the news of apocalypse to its fellow crickets. Hearing the chirped signal, the little nocturnal birds, alarmed, cease playing on the wind above the ridges of the hills and fly hurriedly over to the mainland to announce the dreadful tidings. The news spreads like wildfire.

From the crenellated coast of Venezuela in the north to the sunless southernmost tip of Tierra del Fuego, from the Bahía de Sechura to where the Parahyba River flows into the Atlantic in the east, there is a delicate, high-pitched trilling sound, which takes on a shriller quality as millions of grasshoppers join in. The sound swells. All the bees and mosquitoes start to buzz; from the mountain slopes and treetops and the roofs of houses all the crickets rub their notched hind legs against their forewings, transmitting their rasping codes to other insects across the huge expanses. Everything capable of producing a sound makes itself heard: like an endless, shrill death rattle, the appalling sound soars through the *selvas,* across the *llanos, campos* and *pampas,* over the vast plantations and *haciendas,* the tiny plots of the peasants, through the valleys green from the rain and along the muddy riverbeds, through the never-sleeping streets of the great cities.

When I was a boy, lying in the small square of darkness in my room, I often used to listen to the crickets: the shrill rasp of a house cricket behind the wardrobe, or the enervating kri-kri-kri-kri of a jet-black garden cricket outside. On nights when their monotonous chirping kept me awake until late, I could hear the cursing and shouting of the drunken sailors beating each other up and throwing bottles. Our house was close to the harbour and living in the same street was a lady of easy virtue, although at the time I had only the faintest notion of what that meant. Her house was the onshore address of innumerable seamen, mainly Norwegians, who came to drink, kick up a rumpus and so on. The Norwegians all drank Dutch gin mixed with bright-red Curaçao liqueur, both of which they bought at my father's shop. My father, himself a devoted *jenever* drinker, called the combination of aged Dutch gin and the sticky-sweet liqueur "dynamite." No wonder the wild drinking sessions invariably ended with a free-for-all in the street. The neighbours said that after these battles, anyone rendered unconscious either by drink or by the injuries they had sustained was always carried or dragged back to their ship by his mates; no Norwegian seaman was ever left behind. My mother told me that when I was born — it was early one Sunday morning, pouring with rain, and the church bells were ringing for the first dawn mass before Christmas — there was a fight in full swing in our street. My father had to brave both the rain and the flying bottles to fetch the midwife.

Not ten minutes' walk from our house was a hill on which a large water tank had been built. From there you could look down on the whole expanse of the harbour. I often sat there after school and watched the bustle below. Whenever a vessel put to sea flying the Norwegian flag, I wondered whether the crew, after a night of boozing and brawling, were still capable of manoeuvring the ship out of the harbour without ramming the vessels moored in the narrow channel or sinking the opened pontoon bridge. Even when the ship reached open water, I was still doubtful whether the sailors, with their fearsome hangovers, would manage to cross the ocean and reach Norway safely.

Almost every ship I saw sailing out of the harbour awakened an odd, unpleasant sensation in me, as if I had forfeited something. As I watched the vessel grow smaller and smaller, I felt horribly lonely and abandoned. At one such moment I scratched the words OUT-LAW in huge letters on the steel belly of the water tank. When I lay awake at night, I struggled to understand the strange feeling these departing ships provoked in me, but without success. Until, that is, the night when I was listening to the idiotic sound of the crickets and suddenly heard three sharp blasts from the siren of a vessel ready to sail: every ship is a tiny, sparsely populated island. When it is on the high seas, surrounded on all sides by endless ocean, each member of the crew is a loner, without parents, without a dog, without a school, without a church. His day's work is closely regulated and his free time is contractually fixed. The crew sleep on stiff canvas in tiny one-person cabins too small to stand up in. Once docked in a foreign port, they can go on shore leave, get drunk and womanise.

Yet I had no desire to become a sailor when I grew up. Even as a child I was a coward.

At 2:47 the inhabitants of twenty republics rush out of their houses and shacks. The streets overflow, screaming children are trampled underfoot. In the countryside the frantic livestock break down fences and stampede into the fields.

When I was small, and even after my boyhood was over, I often fled from people, things and situations that I didn't like or that scared me. Sometimes for no apparent reason. For example, I have never found a rational explanation for my determined avoidance of church services, unless it was the annoying slowness of the Protestant ministers I encountered when I was still young and a keen observer. Unlike the Catholic fathers I had watched, who rattle off everything as quickly as possible to the accompaniment of careless movements and gestures, ministers are extremely sluggish and drag proceedings out for as long as possible. With measured Old Testament solemnity, they stride towards the pulpit, mount it with dignity, stare for a few seconds over the heads of the congregation at a blank wall, and then spend thirty minutes expounding a two-line biblical text that is as clear as crystal.

When I did my military service, those not yet twenty-one were regarded as underage and had to attend church on Sundays. I was eighteen, and very much a minor. With the exception of two other Protestants, all the men in my company were Catholics; they had it easy, since after attending a brief mass in the gym they were free to go. The Protestant trio were loaded into a weapon carrier and under the supervision of a sergeant driven to the fort church in town. The vehicle stopped in Government Square, and under the watchful eye of our chaperone we had to walk through the arch of the governor's mansion. Once we had reached the church steps and the surveillance ceased, I would always take my leave of my comrades and march briskly out of the square through a narrow alleyway near the old post office. On the way home I had to keep a sharp lookout to avoid bumping into the sergeant with whom I should have been sitting in church.

Sometimes there is no escape from unpleasantness. I once lay on a bed in a neurological clinic in the freezing capital of Colombia while a gay male nurse shaved off my pubic hair very professionally and with obvious pleasure. I've never felt so humiliated and help-less, but in such circumstances it's difficult to make a getaway.

At 2:48 am God embraces the continent with his gigantic arms; with one hand on the Atlantic east coast and the other on the Pacific west coast, he squeezes with all the fearsome geological strength at his command. The continent creaks from top to bottom.

The great cities, the tall governmental towers and the skyscrapers of the industrialists collapse, and an avalanche of concrete, steel and glass devastates the smaller buildings; the church towers of all the towns and villages crumble, burying everyone who has sought sanctuary in the house of God. Enormous tidal waves smash the coasts and engulf the towns and villages along the coast of South America. Fishing boats, freighters and oil tankers are tossed ashore; thick black blood flows from the tankers back to the sea. High walls of water, mud and rock rush down the mountain slopes, burying every living thing in the valleys. The noise of insects continues to swell and soon drowns out the roar of the landslides and the toppling mountains, a diabolical cacophony that bursts the eardrums of all surviving vertebrates. Cries of pain from men and beasts resound through the continent, but, all being deaf, no creature hears another. Only now do the crickets and grasshoppers fall silent and, together with the beetles, the earwigs and the springtails, they descend upon the emptying forests, where they devour everything green. At the same time, multicoloured butterflies and hideous moths invade the cities in endless swarms and attack the struggling humans and animals; the big butterflies cling to their burning-hot eyes, while the smaller varieties and the moths wriggle, scores at a time, into the nostrils of men, women, children and animals and choke them. Light-hating termites leave their colonies in vast armies, devouring the stripped trees and the timber in the wrecked houses. Stinking cockroaches and giant spiders crawl from their dark hiding places on the forest floor to partake of this final meal.

I shudder at the growing hideousness of the spectacle. I can hear the voice of my Venezuelan uncle saying that God speaks to men through earthquakes, that they shall be visited with winds, storms and devouring flames. I must quickly redirect my thoughts.

From far off I hear music, antique music played on horns and shawms, and very close to me I feel the breath of a young woman. As clearly as if in broad daylight, a procession of beautiful creatures passes before me, their rhythmically swaying bodies immaculate, eyes shining with pride at their nakedness, each with a crown of white flowers, their private parts decked with evergreen. They rise up from the earth and are received into a merciful black hole beyond the luminous ribbon of the Milky Way. My grateful heart rejoices when I see among the chosen ones the long-haired blonde girl who ages ago, in a distant country, ignited my only true passion.

At 2:49 am dead birds begin to rain down on the ravaged earth; only the vultures remain hovering in prayer in the sky. Suddenly they too dive down at lightning speed and plunge their bald heads ravenously into the swollen human and animal carcasses. When the heads re-emerge, great chunks of intestine, dripping with blood and fat, are hanging from the curved beaks. Among the ruins of the towns and villages insects with bloated stomachs swarm over the human and animal remains, now stripped of flesh. The ants leave their shattered dwellings and advance in countless disciplined armies for the final reckoning. The gorged vultures and insects they find among the skeletons offer no resistance and are all destroyed. Once the task of retribution has been accomplished, each ant grabs another and after a ritual death dance each mortally wounds the other with its mandibles and injects its deadly poison. Nothing on the continent is left alive.

It is finished; the entire history of the old continent has been written. And at 3 am precisely there will be light, because the sun will be ignited. This tropical sun, murderous rather than life-giving, hangs in the splendid blue sky that succeeds every natural disaster, casting its even glare upon the universal putrefaction. The vast land is empty and lifeless; only in the deepest recesses of a gigantic ice floe that drifts up from the Antarctic is there a faintly throbbing, slimy mass, from which one day an amorphous, translucent creature will be born. Perhaps one day a new continent will emerge from it. A new territory that this time will not be linked to the north by a twisted umbilical cord and will not have Spanish as its lingua franca.

I go inside; the Caribbean islands have yet to be destroyed. I do not lock my door, I do not let the dogs out, I do not turn off the lights, I do not brush my teeth. I take the pistol from its hiding place in the wardrobe and lay it on the bedside table to the right of my bed. I switch on the air conditioning and, without undressing, lie down on the bed. With fading recognition I look at the familiar things around me: the wardrobe full of clothes, most of which I have never worn; the big curtain over the window, lined with thick material to keep out the light when I sleep all morning; the small, brightly coloured vase that I have been looking at for twenty years and which every Wednesday I am always afraid the cleaning woman will smash, as she has done with most of the glassware; the orange rug next to my bed, on which I sometimes let one of the dogs spend the night when it is ill or sad. The feeling of oneness with these things has vanished—it is as if they already belong to others. I light a cigarette. The smoke I exhale is sucked up to the ceiling by the air conditioning and then snakes lazily back down the wall. Outside I can hear the crowing of the cocks. The roar of morning is here once more and is not to be trusted.

I have no near neighbours and no one is out walking at this hour. Only my dogs will hear the shot—and all the Caribbean islands, which geologists had long suspected are mushroom-shaped, will snap off from the earth's crust and be washed away by the boiling maelstrom, sucked down one by one into the depths by the crazily swirling sea.

Tip Marugg famously considered Dutch "the most beautiful language in the world."[1] Though Papiamento, not Dutch, was his native tongue, Marugg published comparatively little in it apart from a number of poems,[2] book reviews and a dictionary of erotic terms (1991). (Another, a drink-related glossary, never appeared due to his failing eyesight.) Also fluent in Spanish and English, he reviewed, for example, Philip Roth and Kurt Vonnegut. His literary reputation, however, rests largely on his three Dutch novels: *Weekendpelgrimage* (1957; tr. *Weekend Pilgrimage*, 1960), *In de straten van Tepalka* (In the Streets of Tepalka, 1967) and *De morgen loeit weer aan* (1988; tr. *The Roar of Morning*, 2015). Marugg was an avid reader of contemporary Dutch literature and admired such figures as Harry Mulisch, Gerard Reve and W. F. Hermans, though he never sought direct contact with them.[3] He was, however, on friendly terms with other Curaçaoan authors writing in Dutch, such as Frank Martinus Arion and Boeli van Leeuwen.

Silvio Alberto (Tip) Marugg was born in Willemstad, Curaçao, in 1923, into a family of Swiss Protestant origin resident in the Antilles since 1804. In 1949, after completing military service (1942–1947), Marugg joined the PR department of Shell Oil, where he worked until taking early retirement in 1970, eventually becoming editor of the company's in-house magazine *De Passaat*.[4] At the end of his life he was made an Officer in the Order of Orange-Nassau for services to Dutch and Papiamento literature. He died in 2006.

In 1988, having been shortlisted for the Dutch AKO Prize, *De morgen loeit weer aan* won the Cola Debrot Prize, named after the doyen of Antillean writers, whose novella *Mijn zuster de negerin* (1935; tr. "My Black Sister," 2007) remains iconic. The publicity-shy author did not attend the award ceremony.

There are clear parallels of content, perspective and style in his three novels. In all of them an unnamed, isolated male I-figure in an extreme situation reflects on his past and present life as a white man on a largely black island. In *Weekend Pilgrimage* (originally called "Lost Island") a disillusioned office worker, after his usual weekend drinking binge (the "pilgrimage" of the title), skids off the road in a tropical storm at night and while stranded surveys his life to date in a series of flashbacks. He feels that he has no identity. "What would happen if I disappeared?" he asks rhetorically. The narrative starts literally with a bang: "My head lies on the steering wheel. I hit it with a hell of a smack, but I feel no pain."[5] In the final chapter the words return verbatim to frame the intervening reflections.

His memories are uncomfortable and sometimes painful, but ultimately the protagonist decides against emigrating as he had been planning. The balanced, happy life he yearns for eludes him, and he has lost his religious faith and contemplates suicide. But the coming of day brings new resilience:

A glow—old, forgotten, almost lost, but in some miraculous
fashion full of vital force and giving vital force. . . .
This is my town. This is my island.[6]

This conclusion borders on sentimentality, and perhaps its residual
optimism is what the author had in mind when he described the
novel as a "boy's book."[7]

Such an upbeat ending is denied the narrator of *In de straten van
Tepalka*, who is lying in helpless discomfort in a hospital bed close
to death, adrift between dream and reality. A succession of visions
is presented, including those of a hunchback; the child Andra, to
whom he seems to be related; Heskia, a girl he met in Canada; a
masturbating boy (who could be himself); the prostitute Conchita,
with whom he makes love after confessing he is a virgin; and the
peripatetic performer El Indio. Like the soldier in Ambrose Bierce's
"An Occurrence at Owl Creek Bridge" or the shipwrecked sailor in
William Golding's *Pincher Martin*, he longs to escape and apparently succeeds in doing so until he finds himself back in the hospital and we realise that the Last Sacrament he hears is in fact being
read for him. His reaction is understated: "What is left is a feeling
that is hard to pin down of having missed something essential all
along." Throughout the book the connection between the halluci-
natory and the lucid passages is so seamless and the continuum so
complete that the reader is disoriented. Unlike the two above-men-
tioned survivalist narratives, Marugg does not finally tell the reader
explicitly whether the narrator is dead, dying or insane; instead he
leaves us with the voice of the narrator, who has just experienced a

hitherto unknown "inner silence," recalling (dreaming? remembering? inventing?) an evening spent outside the town with El Indio:

> El Indio slowly stood up, stared straight ahead for a while and then started speaking fast . . . I could scarcely understand a word of what he said and yet I knew he was talking about his life, which consisted of little but fretting and in the future would contain much grief. . . . When he had finished, I said something about the mercy of God and he sat down again. We stayed there until we could no longer stand the cold.

When Marugg was asked about his own favourite among his novels, his answer was unambivalent: "*In de straten van Tepalka*. I recognise most of myself in it. It's a true surrealist book, combining prose, poetry and essay in one. I quite simply live a surreal life."[8]

In the twenty-one years that separated *In the Streets of Tepalka* and *The Roar of Morning*, Marugg had not been idle: he produced another long, third-person novel, which he finally discarded in 1981.[9] He also continued to write and plan fiction after the appearance of his third novel: two fragments appeared in literary magazines,[10] and according to the author's housekeeper/companion a novel was nearing completion at his death, though no manuscript has yet been found.[11]

The first of *The Roar of Morning*'s nine chapters opens with a "zoom-in" effect reminiscent of Robert Musil: from an aerial view of the geology of the Caribbean to a solitary man sitting drinking on his front terrace waiting for the dawn and contemplating his past. Only slowly do we realise that he is planning his own suicide.

The effect is repeated in Chapter 8, where we move from a panoramic God's-eye view on the summit of Aconcagua to two horrific atrocities in an unspecified South American country. Finally, at the book's climax, there is a "zoom out" as the whole continent is swallowed up by the sea.

As in the previous novels, the narrative present seems static and the flashbacks more vivid, creating a cyclical pattern in which the unities of place and time are blurred. Here these flashbacks include an episode of precarious lovemaking with a black girlfriend in a hammock, after which the protagonist witnesses a series of riots (a clear reference to the 1969 troubles, a rare case where the historical reality of the Antilles obtrudes). In Chapter 7 the present appears to reassert itself but again is interspersed with childhood memories. A countdown to Armageddon begins, and we realise that the novel's "present" consists of only the ninety minutes between 1:30 am and 3 am.

The book's title relates to the opposition of dark and light that is a key component of Marugg's work. He entitled his collected poems "Horror of Light" and was clear about his own preference: "You can look inwards better in the dark."[12] His own existence tended to be nocturnal, working at night and sleeping during the day. In Chapter 7 the night is compared to a huge, comforting black woman, while the advent of the tropical morning is as violent and destructive as a roaring tornado.

Marugg has been called "the most Latin American of Dutch writers."[13] In terms of content his books, particularly *The Roar of Morning*, powerfully evoke Caribbean and Venezuelan nature and culture (see Chapter 2, where the hostile landscape of the mountain is tangibly present, and in Chapter 4 the scene where the *curandera* places two doves that have been slit open against the soles of the narrator's feet to draw out the fever).

It is stylistically, however, that the latter book is most reminiscent of Latin American magic realism and surrealism. Its ending is unashamedly apocalyptic. Unsurprisingly the original title was "The Destruction of South America."[14] The tone is equally reminiscent of the biblical world of Marugg's Protestant heritage. In Chapter 8 the narrator's repeated phrase "And I see . . ." is a clear paraphrase of St. John's "And I saw . . ." in Revelation 5:21, while at the end of Chapter 7 the narrative moves from a realistic account of a pet dog bitten in a fight to Old Testament rhetoric:

> I rubbed lots of red ointment from the magic tube onto the wound and the bleeding stopped. Of course, I should have hosed the pool of blood off the path at once, but I didn't bother. When the cruel tormenting spirit passes through the land on its tenth circuit and sees this bloodstain, it may pass over my house in silence and proceed to my neighbour's, where it will slay the eldest son.

The protagonist's mystical yearning to "create myself anew" (Chapter 1) and "free(ing) myself . . . from time and space" (Chapter 3), usually with the aid of drink and sex, is a recurring theme. It has been suggested that the climactic hour of 3 am may be an inversion of the time of Christ's death on the cross at 3 pm, while the image of the protagonist stretched Gulliver-like across the whole South American continent also evokes a crucifixion.

The combination of drink ("anyone who reflects on life needs alcohol" was the author's watchword),[15] brooding nature and violence has led some to suggest parallels with Malcolm Lowry's *Under the Volcano* (1947), set in Mexico.

The Dutch scholar J. Oversteegen, attempting to account for Marugg's appeal in the Netherlands, which is at least as great as in his native Antilles, wondered whether this suggested some "deep rapport in the Dutch reader, still in thrall to Calvin, with this attitude to life, which is imbued with guilt and predestination."[16]

Marugg's style, with its substratum of Papiamento,[17] vivid imagery and striking compounds, was widely praised in the Low Countries; in the Antilles the emphasis was more on his sociological analysis of race relations on the island. Cola Debrot went so far as to see the main character of *The Roar of Morning* as "a black man in a white man's skin."[18] This seems very sweeping: in certain respects the character may have "gone native," but his pessimism and self-knowledge transcend race. Alienation, as is seen in Chapter 1, extends across the racial divide:

> The white man isn't white and the black man isn't black; both are aliens in this land where their umbilical cords are buried.

The outsider figures he has created in his fiction have clear autobiographical traits, but this has sometimes led to overfacile identification of author and characters: Tip Marugg was not a total recluse, despite his admiration for the hermit-like behaviour of J. D. Salinger.[19] One acquaintance described him as "secretive but not reclusive."[20] Nor was he a professional failure or a suicide, but first and foremost a highly original, visionary writer and an accomplished stylist.

Notes

1. A. G. Broek and W. Rutgers (eds.), *Tip Marugg. De hemel is van korte duur. Verzameld werk 1945–1995* (Amsterdam, 2009), 669.

2. Collected with his Dutch poems in *Afschuw van licht* (Horror of Light) (Amsterdam, 1976).

3. R. Wester, "Een vreemdeling op aarde," *Vrij Nederland*, 3 March 2001, 45. W. F. Hermans visited the Caribbean and Surinam in 1969 and described his experiences in *De laatste resten tropisch Nederland* (The Last Remnants of the Tropical Netherlands) (Amsterdam, 1975). Although Hermans in his article (142) is generous in his praise of Frank Martinus Arion's novel *Dubbelspel* (1973; tr. *Double Play*, 1998), he does not appear to have read or met Marugg.

4. H. E. Coomans, "Biografie van Silvio Alberto (Tip) Marugg," in *Drie Curaçaose schrijvers in veelvoud*, ed. H. E. Coomans et al. (Zutphen, 1991), 277–284.

5. *Weekend Pilgrimage*, tr. R. Edwards (London, 1960), 5 and 180.

6. Ibid., 190.

7. Wester, "Een vreemdeling op aarde."

8. Ibid.

9. C. Zoon, "De heremiet van Pannekoek," in *Tip Marugg. De hemel is van korte duur, Verzameld werk 1945–1995*, ed. A. G. Broek and W. Rutgers (Amsterdam, 2009), 652. See also Wester, "Een vreemdeling op aarde," 47.

10. "De leguaan en de overlevende" (The Iguana and the Survivor)

and "Groeizame aftasting" (Fertile Exploration), both in *Tip Marugg. De hemel is van korte duur, Verzameld werk 1945–1995*, ed. A. G. Broek and W. Rutgers (Amsterdam, 2009), 427–430 and 431–434.

11. P. Possel (ed.), *Niemand is een eiland. Het leven van Tip Marugg in gesprekken* (Amsterdam, 2009), 119.

12. C. Zoon, "De heremiet van Pannekoek," 642.

13. Netherlands Foundation for Literature, http://www.letterenfonds .nl/en/book/872/the-roar-of-morning.

14. H. M. van den Brink, "De dunste schaduw van het eiland," *Cultureel Supplement NRC Handelsblad*, 2 August 1985. In fact, this was the title given to a section of Chapter 9 published in a magazine.

15. H. J. Vaders, interview, in *Tip Marugg, De hemel is van korte duur, Verzameld werk 1945–1995*, ed. A. G. Broek and W. Rutgers (Amsterdam, 2009), 627–633.

16. J. Oversteegen, "In de val," in *Drie Curaçaose schrijvers in veelvoud*, ed. H. E. Coomans et al. (Zutphen, 1991), 335.

17. See P. Heuvel, "Van aanloeien tot zielstuimel. Over taalgebruik in de romans van Tip Marugg," in *Drie Curaçaose schrijvers in veelvoud*, ed. H. E. Coomans et al. (Zutphen, 1991), 358–364.

18. The Dutch phrase is "van binnen vernegerd." Quoted in J. de Roo, *Antilliaans literair logboek* (Zutphen, 1980), 39.

19. Possel, *Niemand is een eiland*, 25.

20. H. J. Vaders, *Tip Marugg*, 71.

TIP MARUGG (Curaçao, 1923–2006) wrote both in his native Papiamento and in Dutch. However, for most of his poetry and all three of his published novels he uses Dutch, a language that he loved and that in his hands becomes a powerfully expressive tool for rendering his stark and, in the case of the present book, his masterpiece, *The Roar of Morning*, apocalyptic vision.

PAUL VINCENT studied at Cambridge and Amsterdam, and taught Dutch at the University of London for over twenty years before becoming a full-time translator in 1989. He has translated a wide variety of poetry, nonfiction and fiction from Dutch, including work by Achterberg, Couperus, Elsschot, Mulisch, Mortier, Martinus Arion and Van den Brink. He is a member of the Society of Dutch Literature in Leiden. In 2012 he was awarded the Vondel Translation Prize for his version of Louis Paul Boon's *My Little War* (Dalkey Archive Press, 2010).